GRIN AND BEAR IT

"Brain Eater?" Rooster grew grim. "He's the worst man-killer I've ever come across, and I've got pretty near seventy winters under my belt."

"You're sure it's a male?"

"So everyone says."

"You've been out after him?"

"Twice so far," Rooster said. "Each time I came back empty-handed. He's like a ghost, Skye. And he's so smart, it's spooky. To tell you the truth, I was thinking about calling it quits. But if you're willing to partner up, I'll stay and we can go after him together."

"Brain Eater is as good as dead," Fargo said, and grinned.

"You're not listening," Rooster said. "This bear ain't like any other. We go after him, hoss, there's a good chance neither of us will come back alive."

THE TRAILSMAN

#356

GRIZZLY FURY

by

Jon Sharpe

A SIGNET BOOK

SIGNET
Published by New American Library, a division of
Penguin Group (USA) Inc., 375 Hudson Street,
New York, New York 10014, USA
Penguin Group (Canada), 90 Eglinton Avenue East, Suite 700, Toronto,
Ontario M4P 2Y3, Canada (a division of Pearson Penguin Canada Inc.)
Penguin Books Ltd., 80 Strand, London WC2R 0RL, England
Penguin Ireland, 25 St. Stephen's Green, Dublin 2,
Ireland (a division of Penguin Books Ltd.)
Penguin Group (Australia), 250 Camberwell Road, Camberwell, Victoria 3124,
Australia (a division of Pearson Australia Group Pty. Ltd.)
Penguin Books India Pvt. Ltd., 11 Community Centre, Panchsheel Park,
New Delhi - 110 017, India
Penguin Group (NZ), 67 Apollo Drive, Rosedale, Auckland 0632,
New Zealand (a division of Pearson New Zealand Ltd.)
Penguin Books (South Africa) (Pty.) Ltd., 24 Sturdee Avenue,
Rosebank, Johannesburg 2196, South Africa

Penguin Books Ltd., Registered Offices:
80 Strand, London WC2R 0RL, England

First published by Signet, an imprint of New American Library,
a division of Penguin Group (USA) Inc.

First Printing, June 2011
10 9 8 7 6 5 4 3 2 1

The first chapter of this book previously appeared in *Texas Gunrunners*, the three hundred fifty-fifth volume in this series.

Copyright © Penguin Group (USA) Inc., 2011
All rights reserved

 REGISTERED TRADEMARK—MARCA REGISTRADA

Printed in the United States of America

The Trailsman

Beginnings . . . they bend the tree and they mark the man. Skye Fargo was born when he was eighteen. Terror was his midwife, vengeance his first cry. Killing spawned Skye Fargo, ruthless, cold-blooded murder. Out of the acrid smoke of gunpowder still hanging in the air, he rose, cried out a promise never forgotten.

The Trailsman they began to call him all across the West: searcher, scout, hunter, the man who could see where others only looked, his skills for hire but not his soul, the man who lived each day to the fullest, yet trailed each tomorrow. Skye Fargo, the Trailsman, the seeker who could take the wildness of a land and the wanting of a woman and make them his own.

*The Northern Rockies, 1861—where fang and claw
make a feast of human flesh.*

1

The first to die was a prospector. Old Harry, folks called him. Elk hunters were near his diggings and decided to pay him a visit. Everyone liked the old man. He could spin yarns by the hour.

His yarn-spinning days were over. They found Old Harry's legs near his cabin. A blood trail led to an arm and more blood led to the rest of him. His head had been split open and his brains apparently eaten.

The tracks of the culprit were plain enough. Old Harry's attacker was a bear. Judging by the size of the prints it was a grizzly. An exceptionally large grizzly, but then, large bears were nothing new in the mountains that far north.

The hunters buried the remains and went on with their hunt.

The bear was long gone and they figured they had nothing to worry about. They found elk and shot a bull and skinned it and dried and salted the meat. There were five of them with families to feed so one elk wasn't enough. Four hunters went off the next day while the fifth man stayed at camp. The four returned toward sunset, worn and tired and hungry and empty-handed, to find their camp in a shambles and their companion missing. Their effects had been torn apart. The racks of elk meat had been shattered. They looked for their friend and finally came on parts of his body in a ravine. It was Old Harry all over again, only worse. Their friend's head, too, had been split like a melon, and the brains devoured.

The hunters got out of there. They rode like madmen the twenty-five miles down to Gold Creek and told everyone what had happened. It was the talk of the town for weeks and then they had new things to talk about.

Bear attacks were common enough that the deaths didn't alarm them.

Then one evening a horse came limping into town. It was lathered with sweat and bleeding from claw marks. Some of them knew the man who owned it. A large party hurried to his cabin four miles up the creek.

The front door had been busted in. Inside was horror. Blood was everywhere, along with bits and pieces of the victim.

That a bear was to blame was obvious. That it was the same bear occurred to them when they found that the man's brains had been scooped out.

They realized the grizzly must have followed the elk hunters down. That was unusual but not remarkable. They thought they were dealing with an ordinary bear and organized a hunt to put an end to the man-killer before anyone else died.

Fifty men bristling with weapons rode out to wage battle with the beast. They used dogs to follow the trail, big, fearless dogs that had gone after other bears and mountain lions many a time. The dogs found the scent and their owner let them loose and for over a mile their baying showed they were hard after their quarry.

The men hurried to catch up. They were excited and confident and told one another that the grizzly was fit to be stuffed and mounted.

When the howls changed to yowls of terror, it stopped them in their tracks. They sat breathless and still as the screams and shrieks seemed to go on forever. When silence fell they cautiously advanced.

It was as bad as they imagined it would be. The dogs had been slaughtered. For half an acre the ground was a jigsaw of legs and tails and ribs and bodies. They tried to take up the trail without the dogs but they soon lost it.

For a few days Gold Creek was as quiet as a church. But these were hardy men and women, used to life in the wild, and gradually their lives returned to normal.

A couple of weeks passed. One day smoke was seen rising above a cabin along the creek. So much smoke, it drew others to investigate. The cabin was in flames. They yelled for the prospector who lived there but he didn't answer. They reckoned he must have knocked a lamp over and they worried that he was still inside and had been burned to death. Then someone noticed blood and they followed it into the trees. The remains were like a trail of bread crumbs. Here an arm, there a leg, at another spot a foot. The torso was whole, which surprised them. The brains were missing, which didn't.

A town meeting was called. Everyone agreed this was a serious situation. Four people and seven good dogs were dead.

They decided to send for the best bear hunter in the territory.

His fee was a hundred dollars but that was money well spent if they could be rid of the grizzly.

The bear hunter came. He brought his own dogs, four of the largest and meanest-looking hounds anyone had ever seen. He spent an evening drinking and boasting of his prowess and the next morning he and his mean-looking hounds rode off after the bear.

No one ever set eyes on the hunter or his dogs again. About a month after the bear hunter disappeared, two men going up the creek to their claim happened on a dead mule. Its throat had been ripped out. Its owner, or rather, parts of him, lay nearby. He had a hole in the top of his head as big around as a pie pan. And no brain.

Another hunt was organized. Every last man who lived in or around Gold Creek was required to report with a rifle and be mustered into what the town council called the Bear Militia. They took to the field with high hopes. Every square foot for miles was scoured. They didn't find so much as a fresh track.

The hunt was deemed a success. They told themselves that their show of force had scared the bear off—that they were shed of it once and for all.

The next morning the parson rode out to visit an elderly woman and her husband. The woman was sickly and the parson paid daily visits to bolster her spirits. Their cabin was less than a quarter of a mile from Gold Creek. He knew something was wrong when he saw that the door hung by a hinge. Clutching his Bible, the parson made bold to poke his head in. He promptly drew it out again, and retched.

Yet another town meeting was called. Enough was enough, everyone agreed. The way things were going, pretty soon the grizzly would be breaking into homes in town. Something had to be done.

Gold Creek was prosperous. They had six hundred dollars in the treasury but they didn't think that was enough. They took up a collection that brought the total to a thousand. The mayor thought that was piddling. They needed the best and the best didn't come cheap. He reminded them of how many had lost their lives, and how many more might lose theirs, and called on everyone to do their civic duty and donate as much as they could afford. He also threatened to close the saloons until he had a large enough sum to suit him.

A week later the flyers went out. They were sent to newspapers far and wide, announcing that a five-thousand-dollar bounty had been placed on the grizzly that was terrorizing Gold Creek.

They even gave the bear a name.

They called it Brain Eater.

Skye Fargo came up the trail from Fort Flathead. He swung around Flathead Lake and followed Swann River to the mountains. Instead of crossing over Maria Pass to the other side of the divide, he took the trail that led north and in a few days reached Gold Creek.

From a distance it looked like any other boomtown except that most of the buildings were made from logs. At the south end stood an exception, a church with a steeple. There were a few houses, too, that boasted of the prosperity of their owners.

Flowing past the town from the north was the ribbon of water that accounted for much of Gold Creek's wealth.

Fargo gigged the Ovaro down the mountain. A big man, he wore buckskins and a red bandanna. A Colt was strapped around his waist and the stock of a rifle jutted from his saddle scabbard. His lake blue eyes missed little as he passed outlying cabins and shacks and entered the town.

He was pleased to see so many saloons—six, by his count. It suggested to him that like many frontier settlements, the people of Gold Creek revered the Lord on Sunday and raised holy hell the rest of the week.

A portly man in a bowler was crossing the street and nodded as he went by.

"Ask you a question, mister," Fargo said, drawing rein.

The man had florid cheeks and ferret eyes. He stopped and looked Fargo up and down and said, "Another one, by God."

"Another what?" Fargo said, not sure he liked the man's tone.

"Another fool after that damn griz," the man said. "Or am I mistaken?"

"It's not dead yet?" Fargo wanted to know. He'd hate to think he had come all this way for nothing.

The man snorted. "Mister, that bear is Satan incarnate. You ask me, the bullet hasn't been made that will bring him low."

Fargo bent and patted the stock of his rifle. "I aim to give it a try."

"You and fifty others. Our town is crawling with bear hunters, thanks to that flyer we never should have sent out. My name is Petty, by the way. Theodore Petty. I own the general store. I also happen to be the mayor."

"You don't want the hunters here?"

"At first I did. I put five hundred dollars toward the bounty, thinking it was for the best. Had I known the kind of people it would bring I wouldn't have done it. But enough idle chat. My advice to you is to turn around and leave. Five of the hunters have already died and you could be the sixth."

"The griz has killed five more?"

"Actually, the total is eleven. But no. Only two of them were hunters. Another was killed in a drunken fight in a saloon and two more had a falling-out over how they were going to split the five thousand dollars and shot themselves dead." Petty touched his bowler's brim. "Good day to you, sir."

Fargo digested the news as he rode to a hitch rail in front of one of the saloons and dismounted. Tying off the reins, he stretched. The saloon was called the Sluice. He pushed on the batwings. Although it was barely noon the place was crowded. He bellied up to the bar and paid for a bottle. Since he couldn't find an empty chair, he went back out and sat on an upended crate and savored his first swallow of red-eye in more than a week.

"Well now, what have we here?"

Fargo cocked an eye over the bottle at a young woman in a gay yellow dress, holding a yellow parasol. Brunette curls fanned from under a matching yellow bonnet. She was appraising him as a horse buyer might a stud stallion. "Didn't your ma ever warn you about talking to strange men?"

"She did, indeed," the woman said. "But I always make exceptions for handsome men, and God Almighty, you are one handsome son of a bitch."

Fargo laughed and introduced himself.

"I'm Fanny Jellico," she said with a twirl of her parasol. "Let me guess. You're here after Brain Eater?"

Nodding, Fargo said, "You too, I take it?"

Now it was Fanny who laughed. She leaned her back to the wall, closed her parasol, and surveyed the busy street. "It's become a circus. I suppose I shouldn't complain since we've got more business than we can handle but it's almost as dangerous in town as it is out there in the woods with the bear."

"We?" Fargo said.

"Me and a bunch of girls came all the way from Denver," Fanny explained. "It was Madame Basque's doing. She runs a sporting house. When she saw that flyer she knew there was money to be made. So she loaded eight of us into a wagon and here we are."

"That's a long way to come."

"Maybe so," Fanny said. "But we're making money hand over thigh."

Fargo chuckled. "The marshal and the parson don't mind?"

"There isn't any law," Fanny revealed. "The town never got around to appointing one. As for the parson"—she gazed down the street at the church, then looked at Fargo and winked—"he's as friendly as can be."

"I hear there's been a knifing and a shooting."

"Hell, there have been twenty or more just since we came," Fanny said. "The hunters spend more time fighting amongst themselves than they do hunting the bear. And I use the word 'hunter' loosely. Some of them couldn't find their own ass if they were told where it is."

Fargo was beginning to understand why Theodore Petty resented the influx of bounty seekers. Gold Creek had gone from a run-of-the-mill mountain town to a wild-and-woolly pit of violence and carnal desire. Just the kind of place he liked most.

"If you're interested in a good time, you might look me up at the Three Deuces. Madame Basque made an arrangement where we use the rooms in the back. I'm there from six until midnight most every night."

"I might just do that."

Fanny brazenly traced the outline of his jaw with a finger. "I might just let you have me at a discount, as good-looking as you are."

The next instant the front window exploded with a tremendous crash. Fargo sprang to his feet and simultaneously Fanny screamed and threw herself against him. Both watched a man tumble to a stop in the street and lie half dazed.

Through the shattered window strode a colossus. Seven feet tall if he was an inch, he wore a buffalo robe and a floppy hat. Tucked under his belt was an armory: two pistols, two knives, and a hatchet. He walked over to the man in the street and declared, "Get up and get your due."

The man rolled over. Buckskins clad his wiry frame. He was getting on in years and had hair as white as snow. He had a lot of wrinkles, too. Propping himself on his elbows, he wiped a sleeve across his mouth, smearing the blood that dribbled over his lower lip. "You shouldn't ought to have done that, Moose."

"You say mean things, you should expect it," the man-mountain declared.

Fargo pried Fanny's fingers from his arm. "Hold this," he said, and gave her the bottle. Moving out from under the overhang, he headed toward the old man. "Rooster Strimm," he said. "It's been a coon's age."

Rooster blinked and grinned. "Why, look who it is. Ain't seen you since Green River."

Moose didn't like the interruption. "You know this feller?" he said to Rooster.

"I surely do," the old man confirmed. "He's a friend of mine. Skye Fargo, meet Moose Taylor."

Moose turned. "Friend or not, you'd better back away. Rooster, here, was mean to me and I don't like it when folks are mean. I aim to hurt him some and there's nothing you can do to stop me."

"Care to bet?" Fargo said.

2

Fargo didn't have a lot of close friends. He could count them on two hands and have fingers left. It wasn't that he was unsociable. When he had half a bottle in his belly and a dove on his lap, he could be as sociable as anyone. But people who had known him for a good many years, and were still alive, were rare.

Rooster Strimm was one of the few. Fargo had met him shortly after he came west. At the time Strimm had been scouting for the army and had taken Fargo under his wing. It had been Fargo's first taste of life on the frontier and he'd loved it.

Now, watching blood trickle down Rooster's chin, Fargo felt a cold sensation in his chest.

Moose had his hands on his hips and was glowering. "Mister, I've whipped bigger men than you without half trying. Make yourself scarce."

"Why did you throw him through the window?"

"Not that it's any of your business but he called me no-account. Said I was the worst hunter alive and that the only way I'd get the griz is if it walked up to me and asked me to shoot it."

Fargo glanced down at Rooster and grinned. "Did you really say that?"

Rooster nodded. "Can't hardly blame me. Moose, here, is the Mike Fink of bear hunters. He likes to brag about all the bears he's killed but most weren't much more than cubs."

"That does it," Moose said. "I'm going to shake you until your teeth rattle." Bending, he reached to grab Rooster by the front of his shirt.

Fargo shoved Moose. Not hard, but enough that he stumbled a few steps. "No," Fargo said.

Slowly straightening, Moose clenched and unclenched his

big hands. "I told you to butt out. You should have listened. I don't like to hurt folks but you've gone and pushed me so now I have to hurt you."

"If you're dumb enough to try," Fargo said.

"That does it."

Moose was on Fargo before Fargo could raise his arms to defend himself. A fist with knuckles the size of walnuts would have flattened Fargo's nose, only Fargo ducked and retaliated with a solid right to Moose's gut. The punch would have doubled most men over. All Moose did was grunt and wade in with his big fists flying. Fargo backpedaled, blocking and slipping most of the blows. Those that connected jarred him to his marrow. Moose was immensely strong. Fargo countered a left cross, spun away from a jab, and drove a straight-arm into Moose's jaw. It was like hitting an anvil. Pain shot clear to Fargo's shoulder. Wincing, he retreated and Moose came after him.

Fargo was vaguely aware they were gathering a crowd. Someone yelled for Moose to beat him to a pulp.

Moose was grinning as if this were great fun. He held his arms in a stance that left his face and neck exposed, and when he moved, he shuffled awkwardly, as if his feet were so far from his brain, there was a delay in the brain telling the feet what to do.

Fargo didn't think this was fun at all. He was hurting, and he had to end it before Moose connected. He ducked a looping left, didn't fall for a feint, and slammed Moose a good one on the cheek that rocked Moose on his heels. Moose stopped grinning. He looked angry and baffled. Apparently he was used to beating others easily and couldn't understand why Fargo wouldn't go down.

Moose arced a right and then a left. Fargo swiveled and avoided the first but the left smashed his shoulder and sent him tottering a good six feet. It was like being hit by a battering ram. He set himself and Moose started toward him.

Suddenly someone stepped between them, dressed all in yellow with her parasol over her shoulder. "That will be enough, Moose," Fanny said quietly.

Moose was as astounded as Fargo. He lowered his fists partway and stared dumbly at her. "I know you," he said.

"That's enough, I said," Fanny repeated. "Or I will tell Madame Basque and you won't get to have a girl for the rest of our stay."

"Not have a girl?" Moose said, sounding stricken.

"I know how fond you are of Harriet. But if I ask, she'll close her legs to you."

"You wouldn't."

"Only if you force me."

Moose lowered his arms the rest of the way. "Haven't I always been nice to you gals?"

"You have, and I like you," Fanny said. "I also like him." She pointed her parasol at Fargo. "And I don't want the two of you hurting each other over something as stupid as this."

"It's not stupid," Moose said, and nodded at Rooster. "He teased me. Called me a piss-poor hunter."

"Well, then it's only fair that you tease him back. You can tell him you're bigger than he is."

"Bigger?" Moose said.

"A lot bigger." Fanny held her right thumb and forefinger about three inches apart. "He has a tiny little one."

"He does?" Moose's face broke into an ear-to-ear grin. "You hear that, Rooster? She says you got a tiny little pecker."

"You could go around telling everyone he's a mouse and you're a bull," Fanny said.

"Oh, hell," Rooster said.

Moose threw back his head and great peals of mirth burst from his chest. "That's a good one, Fanny. Can I say it just like you said it?"

"Yes, you may, with my blessing." Fanny patted him on the shoulder. "Now why don't you run along and have a few drinks and I'll tell Harriet to expect you later?"

"I will. And thanks." Moose clapped her on the shoulder and nearly knocked her over. Turning to the onlookers, he bellowed, "Rooster is a mouse and I'm a bull!" He strode toward the saloon, still laughing.

"Thanks a lot, Fanny," Rooster said.

Fargo realized he was still holding his fists up and let his arms relax. His shoulder throbbed. The people around them began to disperse.

Fanny leaned on her parasol and grinned. "I do believe you owe me one."

"I'm obliged," Fargo said.

"Moose has a good heart but a bad temper. He's a ten-year-old who never grew up."

"He looked pretty grown to me."

Fanny laughed. "The next time he sees you, he'll probably have forgotten all about your fight. That's how he is."

Rooster thrust a hand at Fargo. "I owe you, hoss. He'd have beat me without half trying."

Fargo shook, his hand hurting from the punch to Moose's jaw. "You should know better than to make a man like him mad."

Rooster shrugged. "I'd had a little too much to drink and it bothered me, him bragging like he does."

"Still," Fargo said.

"I know, I know." Rooster smiled. "But enough about that big oaf. How about I treat the two of you to drinks?"

"I already have a bottle," Fargo said, and noticed that Fanny didn't have it with her.

"I put it on that crate you were sitting on."

They went over but the whiskey was gone. Fargo swore and looked around but whoever took it had slipped it under a coat or gone into a building. He did more swearing.

"I'm sorry," Fanny said. "I forget how human nature is."

"My offer still holds," Rooster declared, and led them to the next saloon, a place called Spirits. It had a painting of naked ladies on the wall behind the bar and a small chandelier.

Customers were playing cards and drinking but it wasn't as rowdy as the Sluice.

Fargo chose a corner table. He held a chair for Fanny and Rooster fetched a bottle and three glasses. As soon as his old friend claimed a seat, he leaned back and asked, "What can you tell me about this bear?"

"Brain Eater?" Rooster grew grim. "He's the worst man-killer I've ever come across, and I've got pretty near seventy winters under my belt."

"You're sure it's a male?"

"So everyone says."

"You've been out after him?"

"Twice so far," Rooster said. "Each time I came back empty-handed. He's like a ghost, Skye. And he's so smart it's spooky. To tell you the truth, I was thinking about calling it quits. But if you're willing to partner up, I'll stay and we can go after him together."

"Brain Eater is as good as dead," Fargo said, and grinned.

"You're not listening," Rooster said. "This bear ain't like any other. We go after him, hoss, there's a good chance neither of us will come back alive."

3

Fargo discovered that when Fanny called it a circus, she wasn't kidding.

Five thousand dollars was a lot of money. To some it was a fortune. So it was no surprise that the bounty had drawn would-be bear hunters from all over. That so many of them had never done any bear hunting didn't matter. All they cared about was the money.

Rooster took Fargo on a tour of the saloons so Fargo could meet some of them and see for himself.

"It's quite a collection," Rooster said dryly.

Fargo agreed.

There were farmers. There were store clerks. There was a bank teller who admitted he'd never hunted so much as a chipmunk but who told Fargo, in all seriousness, "I don't see where this bear will be a problem. All I have to do is point my gun and shoot." There were buffalo hunters. There was a rancher who needed the money to keep his ranch afloat. There were mule skinners. There was a boy who couldn't be more than twelve, who showed up with two cents to his name, toting a slingshot. Fargo was introduced to an Englishman who had brought a special rifle he used to bag elephants in Africa. There were several women, including a mother with three children who had lost her husband in an accident. Out of the hundred or so, only a handful had ever hunted bear.

"What do you think?" Rooster asked when they were at the last saloon.

"I think I need a drink." Fargo bought another bottle and they planted themselves at the end of the bar. As he filled their glasses he remarked, "They have no damn notion what they're up against."

"It's plumb ridiculous."

"If the town council had any sense, they'd send these folks packing."

"The council is hoping one of the hunters will get lucky and put an end to the killings."

"That, and it's good for business," Fargo guessed. The saloons alone were taking in more money in an hour than they used to make in a week.

"Here's to greed," Rooster said, tipping his glass to his lips.

"Here's to stupid," Fargo said, and did the same.

"So the way I see it, hoss," Rooster said, "is that you and me have as good a chance as anyone and a better chance than most of tracking this Brain Eater and splattering his brains."

Fargo had shot black bears and grizzlies. A few times when he had to in order not to be eaten, a few times when he was half-starved and a bear made the mistake of wandering into his sights before a deer or a rabbit, and once when he needed a hide to make a robe for a Sioux friend who just happened to be female. "Do you still have your Sharps?"

"Wouldn't hunt with any other gun," Rooster said. "Last year I brought down a buff at five hundred yards."

"That's some shooting."

"You've still got yours, I take it?"

"I took to using a Henry," Fargo revealed.

Rooster was about to take another drink but stopped. "Why in Sam Hill would you part with your Sharps? You could out-shoot me with that beauty you had."

"A Henry holds more rounds."

Rooster slapped down his glass, spilling some of the whiskey. "Rounds my ass. Why, those things are only fit for chickens and chipmunks."

"I've dropped a few buffalo with it."

"Hell," Rooster said in disgust. "Bet you had to shoot the poor buff eight or ten times. You know and I know that when it comes to stopping a critter in its tracks, there's nothing like a Sharps."

"Sharps do come in larger calibers . . ." Fargo began.

"Damn right they do. Mine is a .52. It's a regular cannon. What caliber is your chipmunk killer?"

"You know damn well the Henry is a .44."

Rooster snorted. "When we find Brain Eater, what do you intend to do? Club him to death? A bee would sting him worse than your girlie gun."

"Did you just say girlie gun?"

"You'd be better off using that kid's slingshot."

"You're full of it," Fargo said. But his friend had a valid point. A Henry *could* bring a grizzly down, provided its vitals were hit, but he wouldn't care to stake his life on it.

"The hell I am. Look me in the face and tell me you're going to go after a griz as big as a Conestoga with your pitiful .44."

Fargo frowned.

"I didn't think so."

More than a little annoyed, Fargo said testily, "I never said I gave up the Sharps entirely. A friend keeps it for me. I use it now and then. And before you ask, yes, I left the Henry and brought the Sharps."

"What's her name?"

"Who?"

"Your friend."

"Go to hell."

Rooster cackled and smacked the bar. "That's the spirit. Between your Sharps and mine, Brain Eater is fit to be skinned."

"Do you really believe that?"

"No," Rooster said. "I don't."

An hour later Fargo and Rooster had finished the bottle and Fargo was set to order another when a commotion broke out in the street. Shouts flew from one end to the other.

"I wonder what that's about," Rooster said.

The next moment the batwings parted and a townsman thrust his head in. "There's been another one! They have him in a wagon down to the undertaker's."

An exodus ensued, with a lot of pushing and shoving before everyone made it out. Fargo held back and waited for the press to thin, then joined the scores converging on a building with a sign that read simply, MORTICIAN. He had to shoulder through the crowd to a buckboard. A man in the bed had pulled back a canvas and onlookers were craning their necks to see the remains. One glimpse was enough for most; it was all they could stomach, and they had to turn away before they got sick.

Fargo wasn't as squeamish. He'd seen freighters after the Apaches got done with them, and settlers after they had been paid a visit by the Sioux. He'd seen a man who had been clawed to ribbons by a mountain lion, and another who had blundered onto a she-bear and her cubs. But he'd never seen anything like this.

The arms and legs were lined up in a row, the hands and feet at one end, the stumps at the other. One of the hands was missing several fingers. The abdominal cavity had been ripped open and torn intestines lay in grisly coils. The neck had been bitten nearly in half. The face was intact but the crown of the head was attached by slivers of flesh and where the brains should be was a cavity.

"Merciful heavens," a woman blurted, and vomited.

"Who was it?" someone asked the man holding the canvas.

"Ira Stoddard," the man said. "He had a claim about two miles out. They found him near the creek. Or this that was left of him, anyhow."

Rooster nudged Fargo. "Maybe we should go have a look-see before the horde shows up."

"The horde?" Fargo said, and laughed. He didn't find it so funny when they were barely out of town and found dozens of others ahead of them.

"I told you," Rooster said. "Each time there's a killing all of these so-called hunters want to be the first there in the hope they'll spot the bear."

Fargo was content to take his time. The grizzly would be long gone, anyway. They followed a rutted track pockmarked with hoofprints and had gone about half a mile when a black horse came up alongside the Ovaro and a shadow fell across him. "What the hell do you want?"

"Prickly, ain't you?" Moose said. "I wanted to tell Rooster and you there ain't no hard feelings about earlier."

"That's generous of you," Rooster said, "seeing as how you were the one chucked me through the window."

"You're alive," Moose said. "Or are you one of those sour folks who bellyaches over little stuff?"

"Little? By God, I have half a mind to—" Rooster stopped and shook his head. "No. You're right. I shouldn't have said what I did. You're not entirely worthless as a bear hunter."

"I've killed twenty-seven at one time or another," Moose boasted, "and two of them were silvertips."

"This one won't be as easy as they were."

"You don't have to tell me." Moose thrust his big hand at Fargo. "How about you, mister? Forgive and forget, as my ma used to say?"

"I never forget," Fargo said, but he shook.

"Why, that's what that British gent said about those ele-things he likes to hunt," Moose said. "He claims they have two teeth as long as my arm and they wear a trunk on their face. But what would they need with a trunk when they don't even wear clothes?" Moose guffawed as if he had told a joke.

Fargo decided to take advantage of the bear hunter's friendliness. "You've been out after this griz before, I take it?"

"That I have," Moose said somberly. "And he got the better of me every time."

"Better how?"

"Brain Eater ain't a normal bear. He's got the painter gift of throwing a hunter off his scent. Hell, even hounds can't bring him to bay."

"How does Brain Eater throw you off?" Fargo keenly desired to know.

"He's smart. He doubles back on himself. He sticks to rocky ground when he can. He goes up slopes too steep for a horse, knowing we have to go around. He sticks to water, too, and will stay in a stream for miles."

"I've never heard of a bear doing all that," Fargo admitted.

"Now you know why no one has caught him yet," Moose said. "And why that bounty is as good as mine."

"Putting the cart before the horse, ain't you?" Rooster said.

"Listen. No one has been out after Brain Eater as often as me. And the more I do it, the more I learn of his ways and the more I get the feel of him. Won't be long, I'll know what he's going to do before he does it. That's the day I bring his hide into Gold Creek and collect the bounty."

"If he doesn't eat your brain first," Rooster said.

They reached the site.

"Look at them all," Moose said, and rode into the thick of them.

17

"It'd be funny if it wasn't so damn pathetic," Rooster remarked.

Fargo grunted in assent.

The small cabin and the ground around it literally crawled with bear hunters. Some were on their hands and knees looking for tracks. One man had climbed onto the roof and was looking for sign from up there. The woman with her three children had them poking around in some bushes that weren't big enough to hide a turkey.

Moose dismounted and walked about bragging how Brain Eater's days were numbered.

Fargo sat the saddle of the Ovaro and shook his head in mild disgust. Any tracks the bear had left would have been obliterated. He noticed that a finger of pines came close to the rear of the cabin, perfect cover for a stalking bear, and he was about to ride around and confirm his hunch when the Englishman with the fancy rifle that brought down elephants rode over.

"I say, Fargo, wasn't it? Wendolyn Channing Mayal, remember? Although most people call me Wendy for short. What do you make of all these blighters?"

"They're a herd of jackasses," Rooster said.

"I quite agree, Mr. Strimm," Wendy said. "They'll bloody well spoil it for those of us who have a legitimate chance at this beast."

"I've been meaning to ask you," Rooster said. "That gun of yours, and your fine clothes and all. You don't strike me as somebody who is in this for the money."

"Most astute, Mr. Strimm."

"Most what?"

"You are exactly right," Wendy said. "I hunt for the thrill. For the sport of it. Elephants and water buffalo in Africa, tigers in India, jaguars in South America, I've hunted them all. I came to your marvelous country to add a grizzly to my tally, and as luck would have it, read in a newspaper about the bounty and this bear."

"Maybe you do have a chance at him, then," Rooster said.

"I can track and I can shoot and I have nerves of steel," Wendy declared. "I should say I most certainly do." He touched the cap he wore and rode toward the stream.

"Not a bad feller for a foreigner," Rooster said.

Fargo motioned and circled around the cabin toward the pines.

Just then a farmer in bib overalls bawled that he had found a bear track near the outhouse and nearly everyone rushed over to see for themselves.

Moose was one of them, and got a laugh by bellowing, "Why, hell, you idiot. This ain't no bear track. It's a dog print, for crying out loud."

Fargo glanced at Rooster. "Ira Stoddard had a dog?"

"Wouldn't know. Never met the man."

The pines closed around them and muffled much of the hubbub. Fargo bent his gaze to the carpet of needles and patches of bare earth. He hadn't gone twenty feet when he came on the outline of a front paw. "I thought so," he said, and pointed.

"Crafty critter," Rooster said. "Snuck in close so he'd be on Ira before Ira could wet himself."

"Or get off a shot," Fargo said. Most meat-eaters did the same. They snuck as near as they could to their quarry before they pounced.

"You reckon this bear is gun savvy?"

"I've seen it before," Fargo said. Bears and other animals were shot at or saw a man use a gun and equated firearms with danger and stayed away from those who carried them.

"We got us one smart bear here."

"So everyone keeps saying."

Fargo penetrated another hundred yards but didn't find more prints. The pines rose in a series of slopes to a phalanx of firs. Above the firs reared a stark spire. "How about we go up and take a gander at the countryside?"

"I don't have nothing better to do."

The climb took two hours. Their horses toiled up steep inclines and they skirted deadfalls and rock outcroppings to finally reach a stone shelf. Drawing rein, they climbed down.

Fargo cast his eyes over nature in all her splendor. Peaks that slashed the clouds. Mountains abundant with timber, split by gorges and ravines. From that height the creek was a thin blue ribbon that contrasted with the greens and browns of the woodland. To the east a pair of bald eagles soared.

Rooster breathed in deep. "God, I love the wilds. Once they're in your blood, you can't ever get them out."

"I wouldn't want to," Fargo said. He could no more take up

city life than he could give up whiskey or women. About to turn to the Ovaro, he gave a start.

High on a mountain to the north was the green rectangle of a meadow. A creature was crossing it. Even at that distance, its bulk and ambling gait and color left no doubt what it was.

"Brain Eater," Fargo said.

Rooster turned and blurted, "I'll be damned! God, he must be huge."

Fargo looked at him. "What do you say?"

"We go for it," Rooster said eagerly.

They mounted and headed north. Fargo didn't push. It wouldn't do to exhaust their mounts to reach the meadow any sooner. Given all he had learned about Brain Eater, they had a long hunt ahead.

Rather than go all the way down to the creek and then up the next mountain to the meadow, they crossed a spiny ridge and wound along a switchback to a bench that brought them to within a quarter of a mile. A short climb and they were there.

"He's long gone by now," Rooster said. "But lookee here, hoss."

Grizzlies ate plants as well as the flesh of anything they could catch, and Brain Eater had treated himself to some yellow violets. In the process he had torn at the ground to get at the roots, and there, as clear as could be, was the entire track of a forepaw. Fargo looked, and whistled.

"Know what you mean," Rooster said. "It gives me goose bumps."

Climbing down, Fargo sank to one knee. Typical grizzly tracks for a mature male were ten to twelve inches long and seven to eight inches wide. This track was nearer to twenty inches long and fifteen to sixteen inches across. He held his spread fingers over the print; it dwarfed his hand.

"Jesus," Rooster breathed. "The thing is a monster."

Fargo nodded. He had never seen griz tracks this huge. Hell, he'd never *heard* of griz tracks like this.

To the west the sun sat perched on the rim of the world. The shadows around them were lengthening.

"Looks like we camp here for the night and go after Brain Eater at daybreak," Rooster said.

Fargo took a picket pin from his saddlebags and pounded it

into the ground using a rock. Rooster hobbled his horse. They stripped both animals and Rooster set about gathering firewood. Fargo half filled his coffeepot from his canteen and after kindling a fire, put coffee on. He shared his pemmican and they sat chewing as the day gave way to the gray of evening and the gray gave way to the black of night. Above them a multitude of stars sparkled.

A coyote yipped but otherwise quiet reined.

"Peaceful, ain't it?" Rooster said. "Almost makes me forget what we're up here for."

As if they needed a reminder, from out of the nearby woods rumbled a menacing growl.

4

Fargo was on his feet in an instant, the Sharps pressed to his shoulder.

"It can't be," Rooster said, rising. "He should be long gone by now."

The growl came again, louder and longer, and from the sound, the bear was moving.

"He's circling," Rooster said.

Fargo thought he glimpsed the gleam of eyeshine in the trees. "When he rushes us go for the heart or lungs." The skull was a poor target. The bone was inches thick.

The growling suddenly ceased.

Fargo and Rooster peered hard into the blanket of ink but minutes went by and no sounds or movement betrayed the beast's presence.

"Strange he hasn't come at us," Rooster whispered as if afraid his voice would provoke an attack.

Fargo stayed silent and focused on the woods.

"Maybe it wasn't him," Rooster said. "Maybe it was something else."

It had sounded like a bear to Fargo, and while the northern Rockies had more bears than any other part of the country, the odds of it being another were slim.

For more than ten minutes they stood in tense expectation of a roar and a charge that didn't materialize. Finally Fargo lowered his Sharps and scratched his chin.

"Makes no sense."

"Could be he was warning us off," Rooster speculated.

Fargo doubted it. Why would a man-killer scare off prey? "We'll take turns keeping watch."

"I'll take the first watch," Rooster said. "I couldn't sleep anyhow, after this."

They sat with their rifles across their laps and resumed their meal.

Fargo filled his tin cup and sipped the hot coffee. He debated saddling up and lighting a shuck. But if the bear followed and came at them out of the dark, they'd be easy to take down. At least here they had the firelight to see by, and the fire itself was a deterrent.

"Wait until Moose and the others hear we saw it and heard it," Rooster said. "They'll think we're bald-faced liars. Moose claims Brain Eater never makes a sound but then Moose likes to claim he knows things he doesn't."

Fargo was raising the cup to his mouth when from up the mountain came a loud *whoof*.

Rooster put his hand on his rifle. "You hear that? It was him again."

They listened but the sound wasn't repeated.

"At least he's moving away from us," Rooster broke their silence.

"Or wants us to think he is," Fargo said. Long ago he had learned not to underestimate the innate cleverness of the bruin clan. They were intelligent and unpredictable and deadly.

"We could light torches and go after him," Rooster proposed.

"Nothing doing," Fargo said. They couldn't track and keep alert for the bear, both.

"What's a little risk when there's five thousand dollars at stake?"

Rooster was grinning but Fargo could tell he was serious. "My life is worth more to me than money."

"When you get my age you'll think different. I ain't as spry as I used to be. My scouting days are over and all I got to show for it was a watch the army gave me and a pat on the back for a job well done."

"So that's why you're here."

"It's hell growing old," Rooster said. "With my half of the five thousand I could get me a small place in Missouri. An acre or so with a house. I'd hunt and garden some and in the evenings I'd sit in my rocking chair and watch the sun set."

"Never took you for the rocking chair type."

"Neither did I. Truth is, pard, I've had my fill of the wilds and its dangers." Rooster sat back and a dreamy expression came over him. "I'd like a peaceful life for a change. I'd like to get up in the morning knowing no one will try to lift my scalp or shoot me or I won't be gored or torn to bits."

"There's no guarantee it will be us who gets the bear," Fargo said.

"That's a cruel thing to say."

"I just don't want you to get your hopes up."

"Too late. They were up before you got here and now with you to help me, they are higher than ever."

"Damn, Rooster."

"I know. But I can't help myself. I'll do anything to earn that bounty. Anything at all."

Fargo wasn't sure he liked the sound of that. "Be careful you don't get yourself killed."

"We all die, hoss. It's only a question of when."

Now and then a wolf howled and coyotes yipped and for a while an owl sat in a tree and hooted at them, but otherwise the night was peaceful.

Fargo sat up the last half and woke Rooster by poking him with his boot as a pink tinge heralded the new dawn. They had coffee and pemmican and were in the saddle and on the move before the sun rose. For over an hour they roved in ever wider circles around their camp but they didn't find so much as a smudge.

With Fargo in the lead, they headed up the mountain. He looked for tracks, as well as claw marks on trees. Bears were fond of leaving sign for other bears but not Brain Eater, apparently. At midmorning they drew rein on a crest overlooking a spectacular vista of virgin wilderness.

"The damn critter is a ghost," Rooster griped. "Moose was right about that much."

From their vantage they could see back down the mountains to Gold Creek. The buildings were mere specks in the haze.

"What now?" Rooster asked.

"It's pointless to keep on," Fargo said. The bear could be anywhere. To go on searching would be like looking for the proverbial needle in a haystack, only this needle didn't stay still and finding it could take months, if it ever happened at all. Reluctantly, he turned the Ovaro toward the far-off specs.

By nightfall they reached the creek and made camp. Again they took turns sitting up but the night was quieter than the one before and the grizzly didn't pay them a visit. They followed the creek and eventually came to Ira Stoddard's cabin. The swarm of bear hunters was long gone.

It was early afternoon when they rode into town. Rooster said he had to go see somebody and they parted company. Fargo went straight to the Three Deuces, paid for a bottle, and claimed a chair against a side wall. He was filling his glass when perfume wreathed him and a warm hand fell lightly on his shoulder.

"I was beginning to think I'd never see you again," Fanny Jellico said. She wore a pink dress that left nothing to the imagination. "Mind if I join you?"

"Be my guest." Fargo pushed the glass across to her and took a long pull from the bottle.

"Where have you been?" Fanny asked, her luscious lips curled in a playful pout. "I thought for sure you'd come calling after I threw myself at you."

"Went after the bear," Fargo said, and briefly told her about his first attempt to track the grizzly down.

"You actually saw it?" Fanny marveled. "You're the first one who has."

"Don't make more out of it than there is. I might have seen its eyes. That's all. Others have gotten a better look than me."

"Who?" Fanny asked. "Not one other bear hunter has gotten close enough."

"The people the griz killed."

"Oh."

Fargo sucked down more bug juice and set the bottle on the table. "Are you working right now?"

Fanny glanced at a large clock on a shelf behind the bar. "Not for another hour or so yet. Why?" She grinned impishly. "What did you have in mind?"

"Treating you to a meal."

Grinning, Fanny slowly ran a hand from her neck down over the swell of her bosom to her flat stomach. "I was hoping it might be something else."

"Later," Fargo promised. "Do you know a good place to eat?"

"The best in town."

The sign read BETTY'S HOME COOKING. Betty turned out to be a stout matron who wore her white hair in a bun and had the sweetest disposition this side of sugar. She brought menus and gave Fargo a glass after informing him that while normally she didn't allow alcohol in her establishment, she'd let him partake of the bottle he'd brought if he promised to behave.

"You won't get rowdy, will you? If there's anything that gets my goat, it's a man who can't hold his liquor."

"Rowdy, no," Fargo said, "but I can't promise I won't get playful." He placed his hand on her hip. "You and me, out back, after I'm done eating?"

Laughing, Betty pushed his hand away. "Oh, you," she said, and went to greet another customer.

"What is it with you and women that we want to fawn all over you?" Fanny wondered.

"It must be my dimples."

The tiny bell over the door chimed and in came the mother of three with her children in tow. She looked around, started toward a table at the back, then caught sight of Fargo. To his surprise she changed direction and steered her brood over to theirs.

"I beg your pardon," she said with a distinct drawl, "but you're him, aren't you? Rooster's friend? Fargo?"

"He is," Fanny confirmed, looking highly amused. "What can he do for you?"

"I can talk for myself," Fargo said.

"I'm Cecelia Mathers. This here is Abner"—she tapped the oldest boy on the head—"and this one is Thomas"—she tapped the middle child—"and this is my youngest, Bethany." She gave the girl a hug and the girl smiled shyly.

"Care to join us?"

"No, no, I wouldn't think of imposin'," Cecelia said. "It's just that I was talkin' to Rooster a while ago. He told me how you almost killed Brain Eater."

"We didn't come close," Fargo said.

"That's not how he's tellin' it," Cecelia said. "He's sayin' you darn near had Brain Eater in your sights."

"I wish," Fargo said.

"He also told me you and him are partners. Was that another lie?"

"We're hunting together," Fargo admitted.

Cecelia moved her oldest and middle boy aside and leaned on the table. "How would you feel about havin' a new partner?"

"New?"

"Take me with you instead of him. Me and my young'uns, here."

It was rare that Fargo couldn't find a word to say but he couldn't find one now.

"I see by your face you must think I'm joshin' but I ain't," Cecelia said. "We can ride and I'm as good a shot as anythin' in britches. We wouldn't be no bother nohow."

"Rooster and I go back a long way," Fargo said.

Cecelia acted as if she hadn't heard. "He says as how he needs the bounty but I need it more. I have three mouths to feed besides my own and no man to help support us. My Ed got kicked by a horse. Couldn't talk or hardly move. I had to feed him and bathe him and everythin', and then he went and died on me."

"Have you ever hunted a bear?"

Cecelia straightened. "What's that got to do with it? It's no different from huntin' other critters. I've shot me a few deer and a couple of coons and once I killed a wild boar that was tryin' to get at our sows."

"There are safer ways of making money."

"Mister, you're not listenin'. We're talkin' five thousand dollars. Or half if I partner up with you. I could pay off the farm and get the kids some schoolin' so they can make somethin' of themselves."

"Where are you from?"

"Tennessee. Why?"

Fargo motioned at her offspring. "Take them and go back there. Find another way."

"There *ain't* no other way," Cecelia said archly, and smacked the table. "Not to make this much at once. Rooster says you're the best tracker alive, and I figure with your help, the money is as good as mine."

"I'm sorry, but I'll stick with Rooster."

Cecelia's mouth became a slit and her jaw muscles twitched. She gathered her boys and the girl in her arms and walked to another table.

Fanny patted Fargo's hand and laughed. "Yes, sir," she said. "When it comes to females, you're a regular magnet."

5

They ate and returned to the Three Deuces. Fanny had to work so Fargo sat in on a poker game. The cards went from cold to warm to hot and he was on a winning streak and over a hundred dollars to the better when a commotion broke out over at the bar. He wasn't paying it any mind until a familiar voice caught his ear.

"I say, take that back, you bounder. I will put up with a lot but not an insult."

Fargo shifted in his chair. Wendolyn Channing Mayal was as impeccably dressed as ever. Wendy was matching glares with a burly man in bib overalls. A farmer from Missouri, as Fargo recollected, another bear hunter. The man had four friends and the five of them were drunk.

Now the farmer poked Wendy in the chest. "I say that any country that lets itself be run by a woman, the men ain't got no sand."

"That is so outrageously stupid I don't know where to begin," Wendy said. "And I'll thank you again not to slur the queen."

"He just called you stupid," one of the others said to the burly one.

"Real men don't let females tell them what to do," the instigator declared.

"You've never been married, then?" Wendy said.

"I was once but she ran off with a corset salesman." The farmer poked the Englishman harder. "And this ain't about me. It's about you coming over here from Great England or whatever the hell you call it and trying to take money away from good honest Americans like us." He gestured at his friends.

"In the first place, it's Great Britain, and in the second place,

I have as much right as any of you to have a go at this Brain Eater."

"Is that a fact?"

"I've just said it was."

The burly one glanced at his companions.

Fargo sensed what was coming. He hardly knew the Englishman, and it really wasn't any of his business and he should stay at the table, yet he found himself setting down his cards and saying, "I'll be right back."

The farmer swatted Wendy's ale from his hand and the stein crashed to pieces against the bar.

"You bloody idiot."

The farmer threw a punch that Wendy blocked. The others sprang and grabbed his arms.

"Let go, damn you. This is most unsportsmanlike."

The burly one shook a fist. "Mister, I am sick of you and your airs."

"Knock his noggin off, Leroy," another of the drunks exhorted him.

"Release me, I say," Wendy said. "It's not my fault that so many of you colonials aren't gentlemen."

"There you go again." Leroy leaned in close. "When I'm done, you'll be laid up for a month of Sundays." He cocked his arm.

By then Fargo was there. He grabbed Leroy's wrist. "Enough."

The farmer turned in surprise and wrenched free. "What the hell? I remember seeing you out at the Stoddard place. Are you his friend or something?"

"I like the name Wendy," Fargo said.

"What kind of name is that for a man, anyhow?"

"Let go of him and go back to your drinking," Fargo advised.

They were too drunk and too dense. They looked at one another and Leroy did more fist shaking.

"Mister, if you know what's good for you, you'll take that big nose of yours somewhere else."

"Yours is a lot bigger," Fargo said, and punched him in it.

Cartilage crunched and blood spurted and Leroy roared with rage and attacked.

Wendy kicked one of the men holding him in the knee and was slammed against the bar.

30

Two others came at Fargo and suddenly he was half surrounded and warding off blows from three attackers at once. He slipped a sloppy cross and let loose with a sharp uppercut that raised the man onto the tips of his toes. A fist to his shoulder made him wince. Another scraped his cheek. He pivoted and rammed his knuckles into a flabby gut, only to have his arm gripped and held. He brought his left arm up but that was seized, too, and now he was in the same predicament as Wendy.

Glowering, Leroy wiped blood from his face with his sleeve. "Hold them, boys."

"Thank you for trying to help," Wendy said to Fargo. "Very decent of you, my good fellow."

"Shut up," Leroy snarled, and once more cocked his arm. "I'm going to enjoy the hell out of pounding the two of you into the floor."

The next instant a large figure reared behind him and a hand the size of a ham clamped around his neck.

"What's going on here, Leroy?"

"Moose!" Leroy exclaimed.

"I asked you a question," Moose Taylor said, shaking him. "Wendy, there, has been nice to me, and I don't want to see him hurt."

"This ain't any of your affair."

Moose glared at the others. "Let go of them or I'll do something you won't like."

Leroy gave a tug but couldn't pull free. "I don't like you now, damn you. *You* let go of *me*. There are five of us and that's more than enough, even for you."

"Don't be mean," Moose said.

Once more Leroy tried to jerk loose and couldn't. His temper snapped. "Mean? I'll give you mean, you big ox. You are nothing but brag, always going on about all the bears you claim you've killed."

A red flush spread from Moose's neck to his hair. Just like that, he bent and gripped Leroy by the shirt and the belt, and in an incredible display of raw strength, raised the farmer clear over his head.

Leroy bleated and struggled. "Put me down, goddamn you!"

"I can't stand mean," Moose said, and threw Leroy onto a table. Its legs splintered, and the table and Leroy crashed to the floor with Leroy stunned and nearly unconscious. Moose wheeled on the others, who were riveted in amazement. "Anyone else want to be chucked?"

All four raised their arms and backed off shaking their heads.

"Darn mean people, anyhow," Moose said.

Wendy smoothed his jacket and smiled. "I'm grateful for the assistance, Mr. Taylor."

Fargo offered his hand.

Moose looked at it and at him, and beamed. "Does this mean we're friends too?"

"Friends," Fargo said, and nearly had his arm shaken off when the big man enthusiastically pumped it.

"I like having friends," Moose said, and laughing, he clapped Fargo on the back.

Fargo thought it a wonder his spine didn't break. Moose Taylor was ungodly strong.

"I say," Wendy broke in. "How about I treat both you chaps to drinks for coming to my rescue?"

"I like drinks," Moose said.

"I'd like to," Fargo said, "but I'm in the middle of a card game." He returned to the table and sat and no sooner was he dealt a new hand than Wendy and Moose were on either side of his chair. "You want something?"

"Friends stick with friends," Moose said.

The game resumed and Fargo had about forgotten they were there when he was dealt a full house.

Behind him, Moose chuckled. "Oh, that's a good one. If I was playing cards I'd bet all I had."

The other players folded.

Fargo glanced up in annoyance. Wendy looked embarrassed by Moose's mistake. Moose, though, was smiling in serene and earnest innocence.

"Hell," Fargo said. He stood and gathered his winnings. "How about I treat both of you?"

Moose made space for them at the bar just by stepping up to it. The bartender brought a bottle of Monongahela and was filling their glasses when murmuring broke out and Fargo turned to see Cecelia Mathers march into the saloon with her brood in her wake.

"What the hell?" the bartender said.

Cecelia looked around, then came straight toward the bar, parting those in front of her as the prow of a ship might part the sea.

Fargo figured she hadn't taken no for an answer but it wasn't him she came to see. She halted in front of Moose and put her hands on her hips.

"If it can't be him it might as well be you."

"Ma'am?" Moose said.

"I need a partner to go after Brain Eater," Cecelia said, and jerked a thumb at Fargo. "I asked him but he's already got one. So now I'm askin' you." She paused and glanced at the Englishman. "Wait a minute. How about you? I'm not particular, and they say you have a rifle that can drop a buffalo with a single shot."

"I'm sorry, madam, but I hunt alone."

"Then it's back to you," Cecelia said to Moose. "How about it?"

"How about what?"

"Aren't you payin' attention? How about partnerin' up with me to hunt the griz."

"You and me?"

"They say you've killed a heap of bears so you must be good at it."

Moose squared his wide shoulders and puffed out his enormous chest. "A heap is about right."

"Then will you or won't you?"

"Won't I what?"

Cecelia rose onto her toes so her face was inches from his.

"Is there somethin' the matter with you?"

"I ain't been sick in years," Moose said.

"Are you serious?"

"I'm always serious about being sick," Moose said. "I don't like to throw up."

Cecelia took a step back. "Enough about sick. Will you or won't you be my partner? We'll split the bounty fifty-fifty. In return, while we're on the trail, I'll do all the cookin' and such. I'll mend any socks you have that need darnin'. And do whatever else you say needs doin'. Does that sound fair?"

"Gosh," Moose said. "You'd be just like a wife."

"Don't get ahead of yourself," Cecelia said. "I admit you're big and good-lookin' but I've got my young'uns to think of. I can't just latch on to anybody. For all I know, you've got habits I can't abide."

"Habits?" Moose said.

"Do you spit a lot?"

"Mostly I just swallow."

"Do you snore?"

"I never heard me snore so no."

"Do you belch and cuss and pick and scratch at yourself all the time?"

Moose seemed mesmerized by her boldness. "I reckon I belch now and then. But I don't try to do it every day or anything. And I don't cuss much except when I stub my toe or that time I accidentally shot my own foot. Lost half my little toe and I'd have sworn that rifle wasn't loaded when I started to clean it. As for picking and scratching, I ain't no chicken."

"My Ed used to always be pickin' lice off and scratchin' himself down low," Cecelia said. "And then he'd just throw the lice without squishin' 'em. If I told him once I told him a thousand times to squish his lice."

"I only scratch when I have fleas and I don't get fleas unless I have a dog and I don't have a dog right now as the last one got old and died on me," Moose said.

Cecelia nodded. "You might do, after all. All right. You can tag along." She turned to go.

"Where are we going?"

"To my room to talk about bein' partners. I've got to tuck these young'uns in. Come along, now."

"Yes, ma'am," Moose said, and was last in the string as they filed across the saloon and out the batwings.

Wendy raised his glass and chuckled. "I say, you Yanks sure are a colorful lot."

Skye Fargo sighed.

6

Fanny was done at midnight. Fargo was sixty dollars ahead when she placed her hand on his shoulder and whispered in his ear, "Ready when you are, handsome."

The night air was brisk, the town dark and quiet save for the two saloons still open. Fanny linked her arm in Fargo's and led him to a side street and along it to a two-story frame house, one of the few in Gold Creek.

"All us girls are staying here," Fanny revealed. "The man who owns it is only asking a dollar a day so long as we throw in free pokes."

"Smart man," Fargo said.

A few of the windows were lit. The porch creaked when Fargo stepped on it. Fanny opened the front door, clasped his hand, and put a finger to her lips. Quietly, they ascended a flight of oak stairs and went down a narrow hall to the last door on the right.

"This is mine," Fanny said.

The bed was small, the dresser had three drawers, and the small table didn't look sturdy enough to bear the weight of a hat. She tossed her bag on it and turned in profile to accent the bulge of her bosom and the sweep of her hips.

"Like what you see, handsome?"

Fargo had done enough talking for one day. Wrapping his arm around her slender waist, he pulled her to him and hungrily glued his mouth to hers. Her lips were exquisitely soft, her curves molded to his hard body as if the two were one. She tasted of mint. He cupped her bottom and she cupped his. He cupped a breast and she reached down low.

"Oh my. You're hard already."

Suddenly bending, Fargo swept her into his arms and whirled

35

her onto the bed. It sagged under their weight. Fanny hooked her arms around his neck and gazed into his eyes in undisguised lust.

"I've been thinking about you all day."

Fargo had been thinking about her, too. Her lips were strawberries he couldn't get enough of. Her body responded ardently to his every touch. He pinched a nipple through her dress.

"I like that," Fanny cooed. "Be as rough as you like and I won't disappoint."

"Quiet, damn it." Fargo put his hand on her knee and traced up the inside of her thigh. She had on stockings and garters. He caressed the silken sheen above and his knuckles brushed her bush. Mewing, she pried at his buckle and his pants.

Fargo sank into a pool of carnal sensation. Fanny knew just what to do and did it well. Their coupling was passionate, almost fierce. They did it half clothed, their need too great to wait. Her fingers raked his back and her teeth nipped his shoulder, drawing blood.

The bed sagged so low, Fargo would swear his knees brushed the floor. He hooked her legs over his shoulders, aligned his pole, and with a dip of his hips, was in to the hilt.

"Yessssssss!" Fanny exclaimed, her eyelids fluttering.

Fargo placed his hands flat to brace himself, and commenced. He could go a good long while when he put his mind to it and he put his mind to it now. In and almost out, over and over, the explosion slowly building at the base of his spine. She crested first in a paroxysm of thrashing limbs and cries of delight. Then it was his turn, and if the bed didn't break it wasn't for a lack of trying.

Afterward, they lay on their sides, her back to him, his cheek on her shoulder.

Fargo slowly drifted off. He figured to sleep through to dawn and was on the verge of dreamland when a sound snapped him awake. Unsure what it had been, he waited to see if the sound was repeated. The night stayed quiet. He decided it was nothing and closed his eyes.

Then he heard it. From off in the distance came a high, keening wail, the cry of a soul in torment. It seemed to hang in the air before gradually fading to silence.

Fargo sat up and grabbed for his clothes. He was strapping

on his gun belt when the cry rose again, only fainter. It didn't last as long.

Fanny slept on, breathing deeply.

Easing the door shut, Fargo hastened out. He heard voices before he reached the street. About a dozen people had come out of the saloons or from elsewhere and were staring off to the north.

"—could it be?" one of them was saying.

"Sounded awful," said another.

"Maybe we should go for a look-see," a man suggested, slurring his words.

"Are you loco?" someone said. "At this time of night? With Brain Eater out there somewhere?"

Fargo spied Rooster leaning against a post and went over. "Did you hear it too?"

"Sure did, hoss. Downright spooky. Whoever it was must be hurting awful bad."

As if to prove his point, another cry wafted on the wind. It rose and fell and rose again, pregnant with the timbre of horror.

As many screams and shrieks and death cries as Fargo had heard, this one raised the short hairs at the nape of his neck.

"It sounds like a woman!" a man declared.

"Or a girl."

"Poor thing," said a third.

Rooster stepped from under the overhang. "You're fixing to go look for her, aren't you?"

"You know me well," Fargo said.

"Hell."

No one went with them. Rooster asked if anyone wanted to and was met with sheepish silence.

Clouds scuttled across the sky. The night was black as pitch. The rutted track that bordered the creek was easy to follow, though, bordered as it was by thick forest on one side and the water on the other.

Fargo rode with his right hand on his Colt. The surrounding mountains were eerily still, as if the meat-eaters were holding their collective breaths to hear the cry repeated.

"I hope to hell that griz ain't around," Rooster said. "He'd be on us before we got off a shot."

The few lights in Gold Creek were no longer visible. They

passed several dark cabins and a lean-to. After several minutes Fargo drew rein.

Rooster did likewise, asking, "What is it? Why did you stop?"

"She could be anywhere," Fargo said. He saw no sense to riding on indefinitely. "We'll wait here a spell."

"Fine by me." Rooster leaned on his saddle horn. "I'm only here because you came and you're my pard."

"Cecelia Mathers wanted me to be hers."

"That gal ain't right in the head," Rooster said. "Bringing her kids here to hunt a griz. What does she think? Brain Eater will walk up and drop dead at her feet?"

"I suspect she has a partner by now."

"Is that so? Who?"

"Moose."

Rooster started to laugh.

That was when a mournful wail pierced the night, causing the Ovaro to prick its ears and prance and Fargo to draw his Colt.

"It came from thataway," Rooster said, pointing at the woods. "And up yonder a piece."

Fargo continued along until he came to a gap in the trees. In the dark it was nearly impossible to make out but there was no doubt it was a trail, and that it was wider than a game trail would be. "Someone must live back in here."

"There are a few folks who live off by themselves," Rooster said. "They don't like it near the creek because people are going by all the time."

Fargo clucked to the stallion. Trees blotted out what little starlight there was. An unnerving quiet fell, and when the Ovaro stepped on a twig, the crack was like a gunshot.

"That griz could be ten feet away and we wouldn't know it," Rooster said.

"Hush, damn it." Fargo's ears were pricked for the slightest sound. He gave a mild start when a tree limb brushed his shoulder. Another almost took his hat off but he ducked in time. Fortunately the trail ran straight for the most part or he'd be dodging trees right and left.

A low moan was borne out of the gloom.

"Did you hear that?" Rooster whispered. "It's the same female. Can't tell how old she is but I'd say not very."

Fargo could have hit him. He'd never known the old scout to be so gabby. Especially at times like this, when they risked losing their hides and a whole lot more.

The trail opened into a clearing. Across it stood a squat block that must be a cabin. The moans came from inside, or so Fargo thought as he warily approached. His saddle creaked as he dismounted and then he was at the open door, his back to the wall. The Colt's hammer made an audible *click*.

Rooster darted to the other side of the door. He was holding his Sharps. "You or me first?"

"You cover," Fargo said, and plunged inside. He immediately took two quick steps to the right so he wasn't silhouetted against the night. He realized it was pointless, as it wouldn't matter to the grizzly if he was or he wasn't. Grizzlies relied on their other senses as much as if not more than their eyes, their noses most of all.

The interior was a black well. Fargo had a vague impression of furniture. Crouching, he waited for his eyes to adjust.

More moaning came from somewhere deeper in.

"Who's there?" Fargo called out.

The moaning stopped.

"I'm not here to hurt you," Fargo said. "We heard someone scream. We're from Gold Creek."

For long moments there was no reply. Then Fargo heard a peculiar scuffling, as of shoes being dragged across a floor.

"Who's there?" he said again, and it hit him that the scuffling wasn't a shoe; it was a body. Someone was dragging herself toward him.

Fargo heard raspy breathing. "Say something," he said. "How bad are you hurt?"

The feel of a cold hand on his own made Fargo jump. He nearly squeezed off a shot in reflex.

"Help me."

It was a woman. Her appeal was made in a whisper fraught with pain.

Fargo reached out and felt cloth and then wet on his fingers. "Is there a lamp?"

"Table," the voice said.

"Where?" Fargo asked, glancing about.

"To your left. Be careful you don't step on me."

Fargo carefully stood and just as carefully inched forward. His toe bumped something. Reaching down, he discovered her arm. He moved around her and groped the empty air. Suddenly his knee banged with pain and he grit his teeth to keep from swearing. He had found the table.

The lamp was in the middle but Fargo had nothing to light it with. He called to Rooster, asking if he did.

"I've got some lucifers in my saddlebags. I'll be right back."

Fargo located the woman again. "Hang on. We'll have light in a minute."

"Did you see them anywhere?" she asked, with a peculiar hiss between each word.

"Who?"

She sucked in a deep breath as if she needed the air to speak. "My husband and my boy. They ran out to help when the bear attacked me."

"Brain Eater," Fargo said.

"No."

"A different bear?"

She sucked in another breath. "Folks say Brain Eater is big. Maybe the biggest bear ever. This one was middling." Again there was a hiss after each word and sometimes between each syllable.

Fargo's questing fingers ran along her arm to her hand. She gripped his fingers so hard, her nails dug into his skin.

"We'll get help," he promised.

She didn't respond.

Boots thudded and Rooster returned. He struck a lucifer and held it aloft.

"The lamp is on the table," Fargo said.

A rosy glow filled the room. Its light bathed the woman, and Fargo's gorge rose. He tasted bile and swallowed it back down.

"God Almighty," Rooster breathed.

She had been torn to ribbons. Red furrows ran down her arms, her chest, her legs. In some places she had been clawed to the bone. Her left ear was missing and her left cheek had been shredded, which accounted for the hissing. Her right eye was emerald green. Her left eye wasn't there.

"Ma'am?" Fargo said, gently squeezing. "It would help to know your name."

Her right eye remained fixed on the rafters.

"Ma'am?" Fargo touched her good cheek. When she didn't blink or say anything, he felt for a pulse.

"Is she?" Rooster said.

Fargo nodded. He closed her right eye and stood. "She said it wasn't Brain Eater."

"There's another bear?" Rooster said skeptically. "Do you believe her?"

"I'm inclined to."

"Why?" Rooster asked.

Fargo pointed at her head. "She still has her brains."

7

They buried her at first light. They buried the remains of her husband and son, as well. The husband's throat had been torn open but otherwise he didn't have a mark on him. The boy had been mauled.

"They've both got their brains, too," Rooster observed as he and Fargo were filling in the shallow graves.

Fargo searched for sign and found tracks in the dirt near a rickety chicken coop. The bear had left the chickens alone. It hadn't touched a milk cow in a plank shed, either. Only the people.

Kneeling, Fargo studied the print of a forepaw. It was considerably smaller than the tracks of Brain Eater.

"I'll be damned," Rooster said, looking over his shoulder. "So there are two. What the hell is going on here?"

Fargo was as perplexed as his friend. It was rare but not unusual for a grizzly to turn into a people-killer. But for two grizzlies to do so at the same time in the same area was unheard of.

"Do we go after it?"

"We sure as hell do."

For the first mile it was easy enough. The bear had made a beeline for the high country. It plowed through thickets rather than go around them and once it stopped to claw at a tree. But then they came to a rocky slope and the tracks disappeared.

Fargo and Rooster roved back and forth for more than an hour and couldn't find so much as a partial print. Several times Fargo climbed down to examine patches of bare earth but it was always the same; nothing. They met at the top, and Rooster swore.

"It's as if the damned critter vanished off the face of the earth."

Fargo continued searching but in another half an hour he admitted defeat and they turned their horses toward town.

"The folks in Gold Creek ain't going to like that they have two bears to deal with," Rooster said. He blinked, and grinned. "Say. I wonder if they'll post a bounty on this one, too."

"I'm not so interested in the money anymore," Fargo said.

"Are you loco? What other reason would there be to hunt them?"

"To stop the killings."

"You're not letting it get to you, are you? We've seen worse. Remember that time the Bloods caught those trappers?"

"I remember," Fargo said, wishing he didn't.

"A hunter's got to keep a clear head," Rooster said. "Feelings only cloud the thinking."

Gold Creek lay peaceful under the morning sun. As luck would have it, Rooster spotted Theodore Petty entering a barbershop. They drew rein at the hitch rail and went in.

The mayor was in the chair and the barber was placing an apron over him.

"Mr. Strimm," Petty said. "And Mr. Fargo, isn't it? Come for a cut and a shave?"

"No," Rooster said. "We're here to tell you that you've got a bigger problem than you thought you had. Or more of one, you might say."

"What are you talking about?"

Rooster motioned at Fargo. "Why don't you tell him, hoss? I'm tuckered out after being up all night." He sank into a chair along the wall and wearily leaned his head back.

Petty listened without once interrupting until Fargo was done. "That had to be the Nesmith family. Nice people, but stubborn. They were warned to come into town until the bear was disposed of but they wouldn't listen. They thought the bear wouldn't bother them, as close to town as they were." Petty rubbed his jaw. "Are you *sure* it's not the same bear? It's not Brain Eater?"

"The tracks aren't the same."

"How can this be, two bears at once? I've never heard of such a thing."

Rooster sat up. "You better post a bounty on this one, too."

Petty's head snapped around as if he were a turkey gobbler that had heard the call of a rival. "So that's what this is, is it?"

"Mayor?" Rooster said.

"I only have your word for it that there's another bear," Petty said. "Maybe there isn't. Maybe you concocted this tale to try and get more money."

"We didn't concoct the dead family," Rooster said.

"No, I doubt you'd lie about something like that."

Rooster pushed out of his chair and stabbed a finger at the mayor. "But we'd lie about a second bear? Is that it? Why, you miserable son of a bitch."

"Here now," Petty said. "I won't be talked to like that."

"You just called us liars, damn you. If I was twenty years younger I'd bust you one. I still might, if you call me a liar again." Rooster marched to the door and swept it open. "Coming, pard?"

Fargo went out and closed the door and stared at Rooster, who was muttering to himself.

"What?" the old scout demanded.

"You're a silver-tongued devil," Fargo said.

The Nesmith family was well liked, and the news of their deaths spread like a prairie fire. So did news of a second bear. By the middle of the morning another exodus of bear hunters had taken place.

Fargo and Rooster weren't among them. They drank and played cards at the Three Deuces and discussed how they were to find their elusive quarry.

"If all we do is go look for tracks every time somebody is killed, it could be months before Brain Eater is careless enough that we get a shot at him," Rooster summed up their situation.

Fargo would rather not spend that long at it, and said so.

"As for this new bear, it may never kill again. People, I mean. Bears don't usually make a habit of it, thank God."

"Man-killers are rare," Fargo agreed, and was refilling his glass when the batwings parted and in strode Moose. Behind him filed Cecelia Mathers and her three children.

The bartender was wiping the bar and hollered, "Hey, lady. What did I tell you about bringing those kids in here?"

"They're mine and they go where I go," Cecelia said.

"I could get in trouble."

"Anyone says anythin', you send them to me and I'll box their ears," Cecelia returned. "Now shush or I'll box yours."

The bartender opened his mouth to respond but closed it again and shook his head.

"Morning, fellers," Moose said. He was grinning and looked fit to bust with the news he wanted to share. "You'll never guess what I did."

"You partnered up with Cecelia," Fargo said.

Moose's jaw fell. "How did you guess?"

Rooster snorted. "It was easy, you lunkhead."

"Don't insult my man," Cecelia said, "or you'll answer to me."

"Your man?" Rooster repeated. He looked from Moose to her and back again, and laughed. "Damn, Moose. When you partner up, you *really* partner up."

Fargo almost laughed, too, when Moose blushed.

"Enough about us," Cecelia said. "We came here to talk."

She turned to her offspring. "Abner, Thomas, Beth, I want the three of you to go sit by that wall there and don't let out a peep until I call you."

"Yes, Ma," the oldest boy said, and he and his siblings dutifully obeyed.

"Now then," Cecelia said, pulling out a chair. "Moose, you sit here."

The big bear hunter sank down as meekly as a kitten and placed his rifle on the table.

"Ain't life grand?" Rooster said.

Cecelia claimed the last chair and speared a finger at Rooster. "I ain't dumb and I won't be teased."

"He's teasing you?" Moose said.

"He's teasin' us," Cecelia said. "But never you mind. He's your friend so we'll let it pass." She sat back. "Now then. I don't believe in beatin' around the bush so let's get right to it. Moose and me did a lot of talkin' last night—"

"Is that all?" Rooster interrupted her, and winked at Moose.

Moose did more blushing.

"Consarn you." Cecelia's hand came from under the table. She had produced a derringer from the folds in her dress, and thunked it down, saying, "Mr. Strimm, I am tryin' to be polite. You're an ornery cuss so you can't help bein' contrary but there is only so much I'll take." Rooster went to say something but she held up her hand. "I ain't done. You poke fun at us but you have no idea what it's like to be a widow alone with three small children, and how hard it is to find a good man willin' to accept you and them. And I do mean good. Not someone like you who'd poke a gal and go his merry way but a man who'd stick. So I'm tellin' you. Make fun of my Moose again and I'll shoot you."

"I'm your Moose?" Moose said.

"You are after last night."

"Oh."

"Well now," Rooster said.

Cecelia looked at Fargo. "How about you, mister? You don't say much, do you?"

Fargo raised his glass. "Here's to the happy couple," he said.

"Now that's better." Cecelia smiled. "And we thank you. But Moose and me didn't come here to talk about us. We've got a plan to collect the bounty but we can't do it alone and Moose said we should ask you two first because he likes you."

"Ask us what?" Rooster said.

"If you're willin' to settle for a thousand dollars as your share. We figure that you two and us two and maybe one more ought to be enough, and that comes to a thousand each."

"I don't know," Rooster said. "I had my heart set on twenty-five hundred."

"A thousand is still a lot. And we're bein' generous, seein' as how it's our plan."

"What is this plan of yours?" Fargo asked.

"It's a good one," Cecelia said. "This Brain Eater ain't like most bears. He's tricky and smart and no one can find him. So we don't bother tryin'. Instead, we make him come to us."

"How?"

"Simple. We do what hunters do all the time. They set out bait. So we set out bait of our own. Bait Brain Eater can't resist."

"You're talking nonsense, lady," Rooster said. "What would you use? A cow? Some sheep? It won't work. Brain Eater likes to kill people."

"So we give him some."

"Eh?"

"The bait," Cecelia said, "is me and my kids."

8

Rooster took the words right out of Fargo's head by saying, "Lady, I've heard some dumb notions in my day but that takes the cake."

"Don't talk mean to her," Moose said.

"Was this harebrained idea yours?" Rooster rejoined. "If it was you should be ashamed of yourself."

Both Moose and Cecelia said at the same time, "Why?"

Rooster turned to Fargo. "Do you want to spell it out for them or should I?"

"Brain Eater kills people," Fargo said, thinking that would be enough.

"So?" Moose said.

"He wouldn't have a high bounty on his head if he didn't," Cecelia said.

"He's killed kids as well as adults," Fargo reminded them.

"What's your point?"

Fargo stared at her. "Don't tell me you don't savvy. The *point* is that you want to use yours as bait."

"They're my kids," Cecelia said. "I've already talked it over with them and they don't mind."

"They're too young to know better," Fargo said.

"We need them," Cecelia insisted. "Me alone wouldn't be enough. We need the kids runnin' around and playin' and makin' a lot of noise. The griz is bound to notice."

"What kind of mother are you, lady?" Rooster said. "You'd put their hides in danger for money?"

Cecelia came out of her chair as if fired from a cannon. She was around the table in long strides and slapped Rooster across the cheek.

Rooster's head rocked but he was more surprised than hurt. "What the hell was that for?"

"Insultin' me," Cecelia declared. "By suggestin' I don't care about my young'uns."

"You're the one who wants to treat them like worms," Rooster said.

"You listen here," Cecelia said, jabbing him with a finger. "This is my one and maybe only chance to get ahead in this life. You have no idea how hard it is for a woman alone."

"Maybe so," Rooster said. "But it's no excuse for draggin' your young'uns up into the mountains to be ate."

"You call love an excuse?" Cecelia shot back. "Because that's why I'm doin' it." She gazed at her children and said tenderly, "They mean everythin' to me. It tears my insides up that I can't provide for them as I'd like to. Good clothes and schoolin' takes money and we're dirt poor. And it's not for lack of tryin'. I've worked all sorts of jobs. I've scrubbed pots and pans, I was a cook, I've sewn and stitched, and do you know what?" She didn't wait for him to answer. "Not any of them paid enough for us to make ends meet. We're always scrapin' to get by. Some days I can't hardly afford food." Tears filled her eyes, and she stopped.

"It's all right, Ma," little Bethany said.

"No, girl, it ain't," Cecelia said. "I'm sick of it. Sick of workin' myself to a frazzle and gettin' nowhere." She swiped a sleeve at her eyes and cleared her throat. "Well, no more. The bounty is a godsend. I'd like the whole five thousand, sure, but I'm smart enough to know that on my own I'll never earn it." She looked at Moose and then at Rooster and finally at Fargo. "But with your help I can lay claim to part of it. Enough that me and mine won't ever again have empty bellies. Enough that my kids can get some learnin' and make somethin' of themselves." She wheeled on Rooster. "So don't you sit there and accuse me of not bein' a good ma, you old goat. I'm the best mother I can be, gettin' by the best I know how."

Cecelia fell silent and returned to her chair.

"That was a good talk," Moose said, and awkwardly patted her shoulder.

Rooster frowned and fidgeted and coughed and then said gruffly, "I take it back. But I still say you're taking a big chance."

"Do you think I don't know that?" Cecelia said quietly. "It's why we came to you and your friend."

Fargo understood. "The more of us there are, the better we can protect your kids."

Cecelia nodded. "Four might be enough but five would be better. Besides, any more than that and the shares wouldn't be worth the risk."

"I'll be damned," Rooster said.

"I was against it at first too," Moose said. "I told her no and that was final but she wouldn't take final for an answer. So here we are."

"We can head out at first light if you agree," Cecelia said. "Me and mine travel light. And we wouldn't need much in the way of grub and stuff."

"There's still the matter of the fifth hunter," Rooster said. "Who did you have in mind?"

Cecelia shrugged. "We ain't given it much thought. You have any idea who might be worth a damn?"

The batwings creaked and into the saloon strolled Wendolyn Channing Mayal, his elephant gun, as he called it, in the crook of his elbow.

"I think I do," Fargo said.

They didn't get to leave at first light as they wanted. Word spread that the mayor had called for a meeting of all the bear hunters the next day at noon. Since there wasn't a building big enough to hold all of them, the meeting was to take place in the middle of the street.

Fargo remembered the mayor saying there were about fifty but the mayor underestimated by thirty to forty. The street was jammed with as diverse a group of humanity as he'd ever seen.

The clerk with his squirrel gun, some Swedish immigrants and their wives, a man in a stovepipe hat who claimed to be a chimney sweep, of all things.

Mayor Petty had a crate placed at one end of the street. Carefully climbing on, he flailed his arms to get everyone's attention. Gradually the hubbub quieted. Clearing his throat, he began.

"All of you are probably wondering why I've called this gathering. The reason is simple. Gold Creek is fit to burst at the seams and you are the cause."

Someone in the crowd hollered, "What did we do?"

49

"You showed up," the mayor replied. "More of you than we ever reckoned would."

"If you didn't want anyone to come, you shouldn't have posted a bounty," someone shouted.

"I'm not assigning blame," Petty said indignantly. "I'm merely pointing out that you have strained our meager resources to the breaking point."

"Your what?" a man yelled.

"Since we only have one hotel and a handful of boarding-houses, most of you are camping on the outskirts," Petty said. "You're planting yourselves where you please. You've trampled gardens. Killed poultry that doesn't belong to you. One of you even stole wash from a clothesline."

There was laughter.

"It's not funny. Not even a little bit," Petty said. "We will have order or all of you will leave."

A man in a derby cupped a hand to his mouth. "I'd like to see you make us."

"I've already sent word to the army," Petty revealed. "I expect a patrol to arrive before another week is out."

"Oh, hell," someone said.

"Until then, the following rules will be abided by." Petty counted them off on his fingers. "One. All saloons will close at midnight—" He had to stop for the boos and insults. When they subsided, he said, "I repeat: All saloons will close at midnight. There will be no drinking in public. Anyone caught with a bottle will be fined. There will be no discharging of firearms in the town limits. Anyone caught doing so will be fined. There will be no accosting the ladies of our town. Anyone who imposes on them will be fined. There will—"

"You going to fine us for breathing, too?"

Petty was unruffled. "There will be no spitting tobacco except into spittoons. Anyone caught spitting in the street will be fined."

"God Almighty," a man said.

"Those of you who make fires are not to leave them untended. We almost had a forest fire because someone walked off and left his fire burning."

A bear hunter seated on a hitch rail called out, "I bet anyone who lets a fire burn will be fined."

There was more mirth.

"Very well. Be this way," Petty said. "The complete list is posted at my office. I advise each and every one of you to memorize it."

The meeting broke up.

Rooster summed up his feelings with, "Did you ever hear so much hogtwaddle in your life?"

"What I want to know," Cecelia said, "is whether we head out now or wait until mornin'?"

"We've already lost half the day," Fargo said. "It might as well be tomorrow." He had an ulterior motive which he didn't mention.

"Whatever you chaps decide is fine by me," Wendolyn said. "I'm just thankful you invited me."

"You might not be before this is done," Rooster said.

9

Fanny had on a green dress that made her breasts bulge and clung to her long thighs. She smelled of lilacs. Each time she stopped behind Fargo's chair and ran her fingers through his hair, he had to force himself to concentrate on his cards.

Along about ten o'clock one of the players lost his last dollar and got up. His empty seat was promptly claimed by someone.

Fargo didn't pay much attention to who had sat down until the man addressed him.

"Remember me?" Leroy asked. Behind him were two of his friends.

"I make it a point to remember jackasses."

Leroy's spite oozed from every pore. "You have a mouth on you, mister. Someone needs to shut it."

"The last time you tried it didn't turn out well."

"Moose and that foreigner ain't here," Leroy said. "It's just you."

"Enough gab," a townsman said. "Are we playing cards or aren't we?"

Play resumed. Fargo paid no mind to Leroy's constant glaring. He won big with a flush and again with a full house.

"Lucky bastard," Leroy muttered.

Fargo was still ahead an hour later but not by as much. He was dealt two pair and bid cautiously and was glad he did when another player laid down a flush. Another round was under way and he was being dealt new cards when he smelled lilacs and a warm hand fell on his shoulder.

"I got off early," Fanny whispered in his ear. "Just for you."

"Pull up a chair."

Fargo had been given a queen, a jack, a ten, a seven and a two. He debated, asked for two cards, and wound up with a king and an ace. His face a mask, he put all he had into the pot since there was no limit. Two of the players folded. A third gnawed on his lip a while and then he folded, too. That left Leroy.

"I think you're bluffing."

"One way to find out," Fargo said.

Leroy counted his chips and drummed his fingers and finally met the raise. "Let's see what you've got."

Fargo laid out the straight.

"Son of a bitch." Leroy threw down his cards, stood up, and stomped off in a huff.

"Can we go now?" Fanny asked as Fargo raked in his winnings.

"I am all yours."

It was a cool night and a lot of people were out and about. Two men were having a tobacco-spitting contest in defiance of the new town ordinance. A friend of Fanny's was strolling about with a gentleman in a suit.

"I sure do like it here," Fanny declared, her arm linked in his.

Fargo patted his bulging poke. "I'm right fond of it myself."

"Are you still planning to go after Brain Eater tomorrow?"

"Why even ask?" Fargo rejoined.

She looked into his eyes and kissed him on the cheek. "Be careful, you hear? I won't sleep a wink until you get back."

Fargo did her the courtesy of pretending to believe her. Patting her bottom, he said, "Neither will I."

They turned into the side street to her lodgings. There were few lights. Fargo was about to nuzzle her ear when some of the shadows moved. He was expecting them to and had the Colt in his hand before the first shadow reached him.

"I've got you now!"

Fargo slammed the barrel against Leroy's ear and the farmer folded like so much limp wash. He pointed it at Leroy's friends, who stopped cold at the click of the hammer.

"Don't shoot!" one blurted.

Fargo nudged Leroy with a toe. "Get this sack of pus out of here."

"Yes, sir. Whatever you say."

They bent to grab him.

"And tell Leroy that if there's a next time, I won't go easy."

Fargo didn't holster the Colt until they were dim in the distance. He chuckled and twirled it and slid it in with a flourish.

"You handle yourself real well," Fanny complimented him.

Fargo sculpted her bottom with his hand. "You haven't seen anything yet."

Other than a chemise that had been tossed over her table, her room was the same. Fargo kicked the door shut and pulled her to him and their two mouths became one. She sucked on his tongue while kneading his muscles and grinding her lower mount against him.

"I've been dreaming of this all day," she husked into his ear.

Fargo had done some dreaming himself. He swept her onto the bed and went through the ritual of undressing her. The dress didn't have as many buttons as the last one. Soon she was gloriously naked and reaching for him with open arms.

Fargo melted into her. Her lips were red-hot coals, her legs were silken clamps. He caressed her breasts and pulled on her nipples and she wriggled and cooed and told him to do it harder. She was wet down below. He knelt and slid the tip of his member along her slit and she shivered and dug her fingernails into his shoulders.

"Yessss. Keep doing that."

Fargo was glad to accommodate her. He teased and stroked until she suddenly grabbed his pole and hungrily fed him into her, groaning louder with every inch he penetrated. When he was all the way she lay still, her eyes closed, her forehead on his chest.

"I love this."

So did Fargo.

"When you get back, look me up. You can have me every night we're here."

"Maybe I will," Fargo said. So long as she didn't make more of it than there was.

Fanny began to move her bottom. "You're the best I've had and I've had a lot."

Fargo kissed her to shut her up. The bed creaked under them in rising tempo as their two bodies merged and pumped.

It promised to be a spell before he could treat himself again so he took his sweet time. They were both panting and slick with sweat when Fanny arched her back and her eyes grew wide with the ecstasy of climax. She gushed, humping against him violently.

Fargo wasn't ready yet. He went on plunging into her while she gasped and moaned and smothered him with burning kisses. His own explosion nearly broke the bed.

Afterward, Fanny lay with her cheek on his shoulder and plied his hair. He was on the verge of drifting off when she spoiled things.

"Can I ask you a question?"

"If you have to."

"Will you be honest with me?"

"Hell," Fargo said.

"All right. Tell me one thing." Fanny raised her head. "What are the odds of you making it back alive?"

"Double hell."

Fanny kissed his chin. "You can't blame a girl for worrying."

"Sure I can."

"Please don't be mad," she said, running her hand over his chest. "It's not as if I'm in love or anything."

"Good," Fargo said.

"But this bear has killed a lot of people. They say it's the meanest critter on four legs. They say it can outthink any man. They say—"

Fargo opened his eyes and put his finger to her lips. "I don't give a damn what *they* say."

"Me either. But I do give a damn about you."

Fargo sighed.

"Don't take me wrong. It's not like I'm in love or anything," Fanny said again. She smiled and traced his hairline with a fingertip. "I mean what I said, is all."

"About what?"

"You are the best fuck I ever had."

Fargo chuckled. "*They* say everyone should be good at something."

"Oh you," Fanny said, and reached below his waist. "What do you say to a second helping?"

"I'm a big eater," Fargo said.

Five adults plus three kids plus two packhorses. Fargo was at the head, and when he glanced over his shoulder as they were climbing, he saw that the line of horses stretched for a hundred and fifty feet. He didn't like that. They were spaced too far apart. It made them easy pickings for Brain Eater should the grizzly attack. He turned to Rooster, who was behind him, and asked him to go down the line and ask everyone to ride closer together. The old scout nodded and reined around.

It was the Englishman who had suggested a spot to put their plan into effect. He had come across it while out hunting for the bear a couple of weeks earlier.

Fargo hadn't seen bear sign all day. The sun was on its westward arc and they had about five hours of daylight left, enough to set up before dark.

The slope leveled and ahead lay shadowed forest. Fargo was watching a hawk circle when Wendy brought his buttermilk next to the Ovaro.

"I say, old chap, mind if I have a few words with you?"

"Old?" Fargo said.

"A figure of speech on my side of the pond," Wendy said. "It doesn't mean you're really old."

"What's on your mind?" Fargo asked when the Brit didn't go on.

"Mrs. Mathers," Wendy said. "I didn't say anything back at the saloon when all of you asked me to join your little expedition."

"Is that what you call this?" Fargo said.

"I call it inspired lunacy but lunacy nonetheless," Wendy said. "I understand it was her idea and all, but really, she is putting herself and her children in great danger."

"We know that."

"Yet you and the others went along with it." Wendy slid a hand under his cap and scratched his head. "And that's the part I don't understand. Going along with her, I mean. It's insane."

"We know that, too."

"You could have told her no," Wendy said. "Maybe not that big lump of muscle. She has him eating out of her hand. And maybe not the old man. He has a crust on him but she cows him, I suspect. Which leaves you, and you don't strike me as the timid sort. You could have stood up to her and shot this whole enterprise down."

"She needs the money."

"Is that all? Then why don't we send her back and I'll give her my share if we bag the brute?"

"That's considerate of you."

"I don't need the money. I'm not here for the bounty, as I've already explained. I'm here for the sport of the hunt and nothing more." Wendolyn motioned. "So what do you say? Do we make her go back?"

Fargo grinned. "I'd like to see anyone make Cecelia Mathers do something she doesn't want to."

"I'm serious."

"So am I. You can ask her if you want but I know what she'll say."

"Stubborn, is she?"

"Practical," Fargo said. "Without her and the kids, this won't work."

"What makes you so certain?"

They were almost to the forest. A squirrel scampered in the upper terrace and a robin warbled.

"Have any of the hunters gotten close enough to get off a shot at Brain Eater?" Fargo asked, and answered his own question. "No, they haven't. This bear stays away from anyone who is after it."

"Are you saying it's smart enough to tell the difference? Exceptional, if true."

"I've never heard of a bear like this one," Fargo said.

"In Africa once an elephant went rogue. He raided villages in the dead of night and hunted people like we're hunting this bear. And when warriors went after him, he avoided them just as this blighter has been avoiding us."

"I saw an elephant once," Fargo mentioned. "It was with a circus."

"Ah. Then you know how gigantic they are compared to these puny bears."

"A griz is a lot of things but puny isn't one of them."

Wendy patted his rifle. "My beauty will prove otherwise. It's custom-made, you see, to my specifications by Holland and Holland of Bond Street." He proudly ran his hand along the barrel. "Most big-game guns are four bore but mine is a two. It's the most powerful firearm there is short of a punt gun." He opened a pouch that was slanted across his chest and held out a shell.

"Good God," Fargo said.

Wendy smiled. "It weighs half a pound, to your Yank way of measure."

"How much does the rifle weigh?"

"Twenty pounds."

Fargo's Sharps weighed about twelve and that was considerable for a rifle.

"It can drop a bull elephant in its tracks but it has its disadvantages," Wendy said. "The smoke, for one. After I shoot I can't hardly see. It's like being in a fog."

"What's the other?"

"The recoil," Wendy answered, and touched his right shoulder. "If you're not braced for it, it can spin you around or knock you on your backside." He smiled wryly. "Or break your shoulder."

"That's some gun," Fargo said.

"It has to be. I've gone after cape buffalo and hippopotamus and rhinos, as well as elephants. All are a lot bigger than your grizzlies."

"It's not the size—it's the teeth and the claws."

"Even there, I've hunted lions and tigers and other big cats. I know what to expect."

Fargo looked at him. "No," he said. "You don't."

10

The meadow was a five-acre oval bordered on the north by a stream and to the west, south and east by a crescent of woodland, mostly spruce with a few oaks.

"Not bad," Rooster declared after they had drawn rein in the center. "The griz will have to come into the open and we'll have clear shots."

"Exactly as you wanted," Wendy said.

Fargo had to admit the spot was perfect. "We have a lot to get done before dark. Let's get to it."

Moose helped Cecelia down and she bustled about overseeing her brood and setting up the camp to her satisfaction.

Each of them stripped their own horse. Fargo took a picket pin from his saddlebag and pounded it into the ground. He preferred a pin over a hobble; in an emergency he could pull it out and ride like hell that much faster.

Abner, Thomas and Bethany collected firewood while Cecelia kindled a fire. She took a coffeepot to the stream and filled it. She also filled a pot for the stew she was making.

The aromas made Fargo's stomach growl. The smell would also serve as a beacon and bring in any bear that caught a tantalizing whiff.

Over an hour of daylight was left, and Rooster and Moose had just sat down to rest, when Fargo proposed they build a lean-to.

"What in the world for?" Rooster demanded. "I don't mind sleeping on the ground."

"It's not for us. It's for them." Fargo nodded at Cecelia and the children. She was stirring the stew, and glanced up.

"No need to go to all that trouble on our account."

"It will give you someplace to run to if the bear comes. He won't charge you if he can't see you."

Cecelia gazed at her offspring. "I suppose it wouldn't hurt to have one, at that."

They had brought an ax and Moose took it on himself to chop down saplings and cut the limbs they needed. A thicket provided the brush for the sides. When they were done it was eight feet long and four feet deep.

Although Rooster had complained, he walked around it and declared, "A damned fine job if I say so myself."

The long day in the saddle had given them all an appetite.

There wasn't a drop of stew left in the pot when they were done. Fargo had two helpings plus four cups of scalding hot coffee. Leaning back, he patted his belly and said contentedly, "You're a good cook, Cecelia."

"It's not all I do good," she said, and she looked at Moose and winked.

Moose blushed.

"Tomorrow we start on the blinds first thing," Fargo announced. He wanted them in position and ready as early as possible.

"You're not expecting the bear that soon, are you?" Wendy asked.

"There's no telling."

"It shows up, we'll have it in a cross fire," Rooster said. "It will be like shooting ducks in a barrel."

"Except this duck fights back."

About an hour after sunset Cecelia ushered her flock to the lean-to. She spread blankets and had them say their prayers, then kissed each on the cheek and came back to the fire. Sighing contentedly, she said, "This has been a fine day."

"Doesn't take much to please you, does it?" Rooster said.

"Any day that ends with a full belly and my kids healthy and happy is as fine a day as I can expect."

They made small talk for a while. Cecelia rose and tiptoed over to the lean-to. When she returned, she was smiling. "They're asleep, and I'll whale the tar out of anyone who wakes them."

"Does this mean we have to whisper?" Moose asked.

"No, just don't do any shoutin'." Cecelia clasped his hand. "Let's you and me go for a stroll, shall we?"

"Now?"

"Why not?" Cecelia tugged but Moose stayed where he was.

"It's night."

"Don't tell me you're afraid of the dark?" Cecelia pulled harder and Moose reluctantly stood.

"I ain't scared of nothing. I just don't see no sense to it when we've ate and can relax."

"There are ways and there are ways," Cecelia said.

"You have plumb lost me."

"Come along, infant."

Rooster waited until they had ambled out of sight before he smirked at Fargo and said, "Walk, my ass."

Wendy was sipping tea from a china cup. "Surely you're not suggesting what I think you're suggesting?"

"She has a hankering to have her pump primed and Moose has the pump handle."

"Here and now?" Wendy said in amazement. "There's a time and a place for everything, old boy, and this certainly isn't it."

"You'd say no, I suppose?" Rooster scoffed.

"I daresay I would, yes," Wendy said. "We English are more reserved than you Americans. We know when to keep our peckers in our pants."

"Prim and proper, eh?"

"Exactly. You're familiar with British manners, then, I take it?"

"I know bullshit when I hear it," Rooster said. "Madame Basque told me you pay her gals a visit nearly every other night."

"Yes, well," Wendy said, and coughed. "Prim and proper is well and good but a man shouldn't be a fanatic about it."

He turned to Fargo. "How about you, sir? What's your view? When should a man turn down an offer to have sex?"

"When he's dead," Fargo said.

They were up at the crack of day. In order to cover the meadow from end to end they decided that they should post themselves at the cardinal points of the compass. Fargo figured they should draw lots but Wendy wanted to be by the stream.

Moose chose the west end and Rooster immediately said his spot would be to the east. That left south. Each man got ready.

The opposite bank of the stream was higher than the near bank. Periodic high water had eroded away the bottom, leaving an overhang. Wendy waded across and settled into a pocket where he was effectively screened from the woods behind him and could see all of the meadow.

Moose ripped out brush and piled it in a semicircle around a tree with the open end toward the meadow. Seated with his back to the bole, he was invisible to any animal that approached through the woods. He, too, could see the entire meadow.

Rooster was more elaborate. He chopped several stout limbs, climbed halfway up an oak, and rigged a platform for him to sit on. From that high up he had an obstructed view.

Fargo didn't go to all that trouble. He chose a small spruce at the meadow's edge and crawled under it. From where he lay he could see everyone and everything.

Cecelia added green wood to the fire so it would give off more smoke and put a pot on. She encouraged her kids to play and make a lot of noise—so long as they stayed near the lean-to.

Fargo placed the Sharps in front of him, folded his arms, and rested his chin on his wrist. Now all they could do was wait and hope the smoke and the smell of the food and the sounds of the kids playing attracted the giant grizzly. It might work. It might not. The bear could be anywhere within fifty miles. But since all the attacks had taken place in that general area, the brute just might catch literal wind of their bait.

The minutes crawled into hours and then the sun was at its zenith. Cecelia and her children sat around the fire eating and talking and making more noise than they ordinarily would.

Fargo and the other men stayed where they were. They didn't dare break cover, not when the grizzly might be close by without them knowing.

As the afternoon waxed, Fargo grew drowsy but shook it off.

He must stay alert. When the bear came, it would be sudden and silent, and he must be ready.

The sun dipped and the shadows multiplied. Twilight washed the browns and greens in gray. Soon it would be too dark to see much of anything.

Fargo crawled from under the spruce and moved into the open. The others followed his example. Their disappointment was as keen as his own.

"I should have known it wouldn't be easy," Moose said. "It could be days before he shows."

"The bounty is worth the wait," Cecelia said.

Fargo picked up the coffeepot and filled his tin cup. "We'll take turns keeping watch tonight."

"I take a turn, too," Cecelia said. "This was my idea, remember?"

"No need for you to," Moose said. "I'm the man. I should do it."

"Listen here," Cecelia said, poking him in the chest. "I'm not one of those gals who sits on her ass while her man does all the work. A wife should be a helpmate and no one will ever say I shirk my duty."

Moose's eyebrows tried to climb into his hair. "We're married?"

Little Bethany giggled.

Cecelia told her to shush and bent over the pot to stir the stew. "No, we're not. Not yet, anyway, but who knows? You might take enough of a shine to me that livin' with me will appeal to you. Until then, there's no harm in actin' like we already said 'I do.'"

"I do what?" Moose said.

"Ain't you ever seen anyone hitched? That's what folks say when the parson asks them if they will."

"Will what?"

"Forget I brought it up."

Night was falling and stars sparkled. From out of the primordial reaches of the wilds rose the howl of a wolf.

Somewhere closer a fox keened.

Rooster came over to Fargo. "I've been doing some thinking, pard."

"Uh-oh."

"Ain't you funny?" Rooster said. "But if this bear is as smart as he seems to be, he won't show himself during the day. He'll wait until night when most of us are asleep and he can sneak in close."

"That's what I would do if I was him."

"So when we're keeping watch tonight, we'll be in more danger than we were all day."

"A lot more."

"Well, damn," Rooster said.

11

Fargo's turn was the last two hours before daylight. He woke feeling sluggish when Moose poked him with a finger as thick as a spike.

"Time to get up, sleepyhead," Moose joked, whispering so as not to wake the others.

The men had spread their blankets in front of the lean-to. Cecelia and the children slept under it. Anything that came at them had to get through Fargo and the others first.

"Did you see or hear anything?" Fargo asked as he stretched and shook his head to try and clear it.

"It's been quiet as can be," Moose said. He sank onto his blanket and lay on his back with his rifle against his side. "The only problem I had was staying awake."

Fargo stiffly rose and stepped to the fire. The crackling flames cast a glow that lit the lean-to and the horses. All else was ink. The woods were a black wall. He could hear the gurgle of the stream but couldn't see it.

Sitting cross-legged, Fargo placed the Sharps in his lap and poured himself a cup of coffee. He needed it badly. His muscles felt sore, which puzzled him since he hadn't done anything strenuous. And his head was mush. It took two cups to bring him to where he felt halfway normal.

Occasionally a coyote or a wolf raised a lament to the heavens but otherwise the night was quiet.

Soon snoring came from the lean-to; Moose had fallen asleep.

Fargo refilled his cup and shook the pot. There wasn't much left. He must make more before dawn.

Far to the west a mountain lion screamed. It woke several of the horses. They pricked their ears and one stamped a hoof but after a while they dozed.

Half an hour went by and Fargo was close to dozing, too. Again and again he shook himself. Once he slapped his cheek. It was so unlike him. He attributed it to his feeling awful, and began to wonder if he was coming down with something.

Then, in the woods to the south, a twig snapped.

Fargo was instantly alert. Twigs didn't break on their own. Several of the horses had raised their heads and were listening, the Ovaro among them. He put both hands on the Sharps. Something was out there. But it didn't have to be a meat-eater. It could be a deer, an elk, anything. He added wood to the fire. The flames rose and the light spread a little farther but not far enough to reach the forest.

No other sounds came out of the dark. Fargo relaxed and sat back. He was about to drain the last of the coffee when he noticed that the Ovaro was staring to the west. He saw only darkness. The stallion was slowly moving its head, as if whatever was out there was circling.

Fargo rose and went over. "What is it, boy?" he whispered. He peered hard but still saw nothing.

The Ovaro nickered, and at the limit of the light, eyes appeared. Large eyes, gleaming with shine from the fire, fixed on their camp.

Fargo couldn't be sure they were a bear's eyes. But he pressed the Sharps to his shoulder and curled his thumb around the hammer.

The eyes blinked, and moved. Not toward him but toward the stream.

An animal come to drink, Fargo guessed. The eyes blinked again and were gone. He heard the thud of what might be hooves and then a splash.

The Ovaro lowered its head.

Fargo took that as a sign all was well and returned to the fire. He still had over an hour to go. He finished the last of the coffee and set his cup down. His stomach grumbled and he was rising to go to his saddlebags for some pemmican when eyes appeared to the south. He stopped and brought up the Sharps. Whatever the thing was, it was just beyond the ring of firelight. The eyes stared at him without blinking. He was sure this time.

It was a bear.

He aimed between the eyes but didn't shoot. It was a bear,

yes, but was it *the* bear? Was it Brain Eater? He didn't think so. The eyes weren't high enough off the ground. It might be the other bear, the one that killed the Nesmith family. What was it the woman told him? The bear that attacked them was middling. The eyes staring at him were those of a bear that size.

The Ovaro nickered.

Fargo glanced at it, expecting to see it staring at the eyes to the southwest. But no. The stallion was staring to the *northwest*. He risked a quick look.

Another pair of eyes was fixed on him with baleful intensity. Larger eyes. Eyes that were much higher off the ground. Eyes that could only belong to one animal.

Brain Eater, Fargo thought, and a tingle ran down his spine. He had a bear to the right of him and a bear to the left. If they charged he couldn't possibly drop both before they reached him. He swung the muzzle of the Sharps from one to the other. They went on staring, and it occurred to him that they weren't staring at him; they were staring at each other.

Suddenly Brain Eater made a *whuff* sound and its eyes were gone. Brush crackled.

Fargo turned toward the smaller bear. It, too, had slipped away. He let out the breath he had been holding and stood rigid with expectation but nothing happened. The night stayed quiet. Both bears were apparently gone.

Fargo lowered the Sharps and expressed his bewilderment with, "What the hell?"

Everyone shared his bewilderment. They sat around the fire eating their breakfast of oatmeal that Cecelia made and drinking coffee sweetened with sugar.

"Two bears?" Moose said, and slurped as he took a sip. "That ain't good."

"I've done some research on these grizzlies of yours," Wendy said, "and I was told they're not very social. It's unusual to have two bears roaming together—isn't that right?"

"Unless it's a mother and a cub," Rooster said. "But this second bear seems a mite big to be a cub."

"I've seen a dozen bears in a river at the same time after salmon," Fargo mentioned. "They always give each other a lot of space. If one gets too close to another, a fight breaks out."

"Why didn't these two fight?" Moose wondered. "You'd think the big one wouldn't want the little one anywhere around."

"You men," Cecelia said. "So what if there's two? It's the big one we're after. It's the big one the bounty is on. And now we know that it knows we're here." She beamed. "It'll come back, and when it does, the money is ours."

"Don't get ahead of yourself, woman," Rooster said. "We have to kill it first."

"Do you other chaps think it will come back?" Wendy asked.

All eyes turned to Fargo. By unspoken consent he had become unofficial leader, in part because he had more experience than any of them in the wilds, and in part because he had an iron edge about him, a force to his personality that they respected.

"I think it will come back," Fargo answered. "The question is, when? We can't let down our guard."

"What I don't get," Moose said, and slurped some more, "is why the critter didn't attack us last night."

"You and me, both," Rooster said. "This thing has killed upwards of fifteen people. I figured it would attack us on sight."

"A normal bear might but this bear isn't normal," Fargo said.

"So what do you propose we do?" Wendy asked. "Go to our blinds and wait?"

"What else can you do?" Cecelia said. "You sure can't go traipsin' off after it and leave me and mine to fend for ourselves."

"I'd never leave you alone," Moose assured her.

"But it wouldn't hurt if one of us went," Fargo proposed, "and since I'm the best tracker, it should be me. I'll try to find where Brain Eater went, and if I get a shot, I'll take it."

"Just so you remember that no matters who kills it, we all get our share of the bounty," Cecelia said.

"You and your bounty money," Rooster told her.

Cecelia gestured at her three young ones, who were hungrily eating their oatmeal. "When you have kids, old man, then you can criticize."

Moose stopped slurping to say, "You leave her be, Rooster—you hear me? You pick on her too much."

"Thank you, handsome," Cecelia said.

"Who are you talking to?" Moose asked.

"You," Cecelia said.

"Oh. No one's ever called me that before. Mostly folks say I'm sort of ugly."

"Not to me," Cecelia said. "To me you're the handsomest man alive."

"Gosh."

Fargo had finished eating, and stood. "I'll head right out. If I can't pick up the trail I should be back by noon or so."

"Be careful, pard," Rooster cautioned. "You said it yourself. Brain Eater ain't normal."

Fargo carried his saddle blanket, saddle and bridle to the Ovaro. He threw on the blanket and smoothed it, then swung the saddle up and over and bent to the cinch. He pulled out the picket pin and put it in his saddlebag. He was about to fork leather when Cecelia came over.

"Before you head out there's somethin' I need to say."

"About?"

Cecelia gazed at the men at the fire, and her kids, and then at the deep shadows in the woods that had yet to be dispelled by the rising sun. "This hunt was my idea. I saw it as the best way to get the money I need."

"You've made that plain," Fargo said, impatient to be under way.

"You didn't have to go along with it. None of you did. But I'm powerful glad you did. Without all of you, this wouldn't work."

"What are you trying to say?"

"That I'm grateful and I would take it poorly if anythin' was to happen to you."

"Thanks," Fargo said. Her sincerity touched him. He saw that she was slightly embarrassed by her admission so he grinned and said, "I'd hug you but Moose would try to beat me to a pulp."

"He's a good man," Cecelia said. "He doesn't have much between the ears but the good counts for more than that."

"You have plenty between yours so the two of you will come out even."

Cecelia held out her hand. "Like Rooster said, you be careful out there."

"Always." Fargo climbed on and held the Sharps in front of him. As he tapped his spurs he tried not to dwell on the fact that a man could be as careful as he could be and still end up in a bear's belly.

12

As the forest and the shadows closed around Fargo, so did a deep silence. Usually the songbirds started a new day singing in exuberance. Not one was singing today.

Fargo rode with every nerve tingling. Grizzlies were notorious for ambushing their prey. They were also cunning at concealing themselves. He searched in a loop. The ground was hard and there were plenty of pine needles to cushion the bear's great weight but he found a partial print and then broken brush, enough to tell him the giant bear had headed west.

Fargo went slowly, as much to keep from being jumped as to not miss any of the spoor. Tracking was often painstaking; with grizzlies it was more so.

From the spacing between prints, Fargo deduced that the griz had been moving at a fast pace. It made no attempt to hide its passage and for over an hour Fargo made good time. Then he crested a rise. Below spread a granite slope sprinkled with scattered pockets of bare earth. Dismounting, he checked the bare patches first but he didn't find a single print. It was possible the bear's claws had scraped the granite here and there but the nicks would be slight and hard to find.

His only other recourse was to descend to the bottom and search for sign there. He rode back and forth for half an hour, but nothing. It was as if the grizzly had vanished into thin air. He ranged farther and came on a smudge but he couldn't say whether the bear made it. He scoured the vicinity and found no other marks.

Fargo was getting nowhere. Frustrated, he returned to the granite slope. Maybe the bear hadn't come all the way down. Maybe it had changed direction again. He reined to the right and spent another twenty minutes looking, without success. Swinging around to the left, he discovered a large pine that bore fresh claw marks.

"Thank you, bear," Fargo said with a grin. He examined them; they were wider and deeper than any he'd ever run across.

He went a little way and found where the grizzly had urinated. Dismounting, he tried to tell if the urine came from under the bear or from behind it. If from under, the bear was a male. Females usually squatted, and the urine was usually behind them. But there were no clear prints to go by.

Brain Eater had gone north for about a hundred yards and turned due west again. Shortly after, the tracks pointed to the south. To someone unfamiliar with bears it would seem the grizzly was wandering all over the place. Fargo knew better. Brain Eater was doing what bears always did; they followed their nose. Bears relied on their sense of smell more than any other faculty.

Fargo hoped Brain Eater found something to eat. A gorged bear would lay up after eating. Twice he lost the sign but found it again. The few tracks of the bear's whole paws were marvels; Bear Eater was as third again as big as most grizzlies.

Fargo was so engrossed in the spoor that when he flushed a gray fox, it startled him. It startled the fox, too; the animal bounded away and never looked back.

Noon came and went and Fargo had yet to catch a glimpse of his quarry. He was thinking of that when he came out of a stand of firs, and there, on a shelf not fifty feet above him, was Brain Eater.

The grizzly had heard him and they set eyes on each other at the same instant.

Fargo drew rein.

Brain Eater reared.

Astonishment rooted Fargo. The thing was gigantic. It uttered a menacing growl. Recovering his wits, he jerked the Sharps to his shoulder. Belatedly, he realized that Brain Eater was a female, not a male as everyone assumed, which made the bear's immense size all the more remarkable. Usually males were larger than females.

Fargo took aim. He centered the sights for a lung shot and started to thumb back the hammer. Brain Eater had other ideas; she dropped onto all fours and hurtled down the shelf toward him.

Fargo did the only thing he could. Hauling on the reins, he fled. He used his spurs and the Ovaro was at a gallop in a few bounds. He ducked to avoid having his head taken off by a low limb, shifted to keep from being swept from the saddle by another.

Fargo didn't need to look back to know the grizzly was hard after them. The wheezing bellows of its breaths were proof enough. He looked anyway.

Brain Eater was swift of paw. Grizzlies always seemed ponderous until they exploded into motion. Over short distances they were faster than a horse but they lacked stamina. If he could keep ahead of it for half a mile or so, it would likely tire and give up the chase.

That half a mile soon felt like ten.

Fargo burst out of the trees and across a grassy tract. The Ovaro increased its speed—but so did the grizzly. It was only a dozen feet behind them, its muscles rippling under its hairy hide, its paws striking the ground in sledgehammer cadence. He shuddered to think of the consequences should the stallion go down. The bear would be on them in a heartbeat, and he would be ripped to pieces before he got off a shot.

Fargo wished he could shove the Sharps into the saddle scabbard so he'd have both hands free for riding. He was half tempted to twist in the saddle and fire but common sense checked the impulse. To hit a moving target from a galloping horse was more luck than anything. Even if he hit it he might not kill it, and wounded grizzlies were fiercely vengeful.

Woods loomed. Not daring to slow, Fargo plunged into them. Spruce were all around him. Limbs whipped past his face and snatched at his buckskins. His cheek stung and his shoulder was jarred. Then the trees thinned and Fargo was in the open again. But not for long. A belt of aspens spread before him.

Fargo steeled himself. Aspens grew close together. So close, threading a horse through them was a challenge. He'd have to constantly shift and turn, and ride slower. The only consolation, if it could be called that, was that the grizzly would have to go slower, too.

Another moment and Fargo was in among the pale boles and trembling leaves. Tightening his hold on the Sharps, he reined right, left, right again. Behind him the grizzly snarled, sounding terribly near. Fargo risked a glance and his blood became ice in his veins.

Brain Eater was almost on top of them, her slavering maw gaping wide to bite. Another instant, and the bear would sink her fangs into the Ovaro's leg.

Fargo reined sharply aside. The grizzly, intent on the stallion, snapped and missed—and slammed into a tree with so much force that the slender bole shattered. Brain Eater pitched headlong. Roaring in baffled rage, she heaved onto all fours and resumed the chase.

Fargo had gained about twenty yards. It wasn't much but if he could maintain the lead over the next few minutes, he could elude her. Bending low, he was finally able to shove the Sharps into the scabbard.

Brain Eater was a tornado in fur. Fueled by the fury of her fall, she came on more swiftly than ever.

Fargo broke out of the aspens. Below spread a rocky slope with scattered scrub brush. The peal of the stallion's hooves on the rock was like the ring of a blacksmith's hammer on an anvil.

A band of talus edged the bottom. Only eight feet across it was nonetheless a peril. Talus was as treacherous for a horse as ice was for a person.

Fargo couldn't go around. He'd have to try to cross and hope for the best. He angled toward where the talus appeared to be narrowest and was almost across when rocks cascaded from under the stallion's rear legs and they buckled. Fargo expected to crash down but the Ovaro recovered and galloped into more woods.

Grizzlies had a justly deserved reputation for being tenacious. Brain Eater was a living example. She crashed through everything in her path. Obstacles were so much paper, to be shredded or barreled through.

Out of nowhere a gully appeared. Fargo raced along the rim, pebbles flying. Forty feet away the gully turned at a right angle. He had no recourse but to jump it. The Ovaro never broke stride. He nearly lost his hat when the stallion launched itself.

Brain Eater didn't try to jump. Barreling headlong down one side and up the other, the bear shot out of the gully as if flung by a catapult. As it cleared the crest it roared.

Fargo was growing worried. The bear didn't show sign of slowing.

The Ovaro came to the base of a steep hill and thundered up it. Fargo was elated to find he was gaining. He reached the crest— and drew sharp rein. He had misjudged. It wasn't a hill. Erosion had worn the other side away, leaving a forty foot drop that overlooked a small lake.

Brain Eater charged up the slope.

Fargo had nowhere to go. Once again he was left with no recourse. A jab of his spurs, and the stallion bounded to the edge, and over. Kicking free of the stirrups, Fargo pushed clear. He cleaved the water in a dive that propelled him under. His hat came off and he grabbed it. Angling toward the light, he stroked and kicked. His buckskins and his boots hampered him.

A few more strokes and the sun was warm on his face. He sucked air into his lungs while treading water.

The Ovaro was swimming toward shore.

Brain Eater was at the bluff's rim, staring down at them. Rearing onto her hind legs, she roared.

Fargo swam. He thought she might jump in after him but she stood there staring until his legs brushed the bottom and he wearily staggered out of the lake and sprawled on solid ground.

Brain Eater raised a giant paw and swatted the air as if it were his head, then dropped onto all fours and lumbered into the forest.

Fargo wouldn't put it past her to circle the lake. Regaining his feet, he shuffled to the stallion. His boots squished with every step. He made sure the Sharps was still in the scabbard, forked leather, and fanned the breeze.

The dunking had soaked him to the skin. His buckskins were drenched. His saddle, his saddlebags, everything was wet. He needed to start a fire and dry out but that would have to wait. It wasn't safe to stop until he put a lot of miles between Brain Eater and himself.

Fargo reflected on how Brain Eater almost had him. He owed his life to the Ovaro—yet again. He gave the stallion a pat. Later he would strip it and rub it down and see that the stallion had plenty to drink and ample rest.

Now that Fargo had seen Brain Eater with his own eyes, he had a better idea of what the people of Gold Creek were up against. He'd known the bear was big. He just hadn't appreciated *how* big.

Fargo wasn't so sure that luring it to the meadow was a good idea. Cecelia didn't realize the degree of danger she and her brood were in.

A low growl punctured Fargo's reverie. He glanced behind him, thinking Brain Eater was after him again, but nothing was there. The growl was repeated, off to his right, and he swiveled, his hand swooping to his Colt.

It was a bear, all right.

But a different one.

13

Fargo drew rein. He remembered the two sets of eyes at the meadow. He remembered Mrs. Nesmith saying that the bear that killed her family wasn't Brain Eater, but smaller. This one had a lighter coat, especially around the head and neck. It also had razor teeth and claws as long as Fargo's fingers. When it growled again and moved toward him, he flew for his life.

He wanted to beat his head against a tree for being so careless. He'd been so deep in thought, he hadn't noticed it until he was much too close.

This new bear was quicker than Brain Eater and was after them like a hound let off the leash after a coon. It roared as it charged. A raking paw nearly caught the Ovaro.

Fargo swore. Slicking the Colt, he twisted and fired. The slug drilled the ground in front of the grizzly. He thumbed back the hammer to shoot again but the bear veered and broke off the chase and disappeared into the undergrowth.

Some bears were scared of guns; the noise sent them scurrying.

Fargo didn't stop. He had escaped two bears in as many minutes and he would be damned if he would push his luck. He stayed at a gallop until he was sure neither was after him.

It was a long ride to the meadow and his friends. The sun had been down for more than an hour when the glow of their fire told him he didn't have far to go.

Rooster was the first to spot him, and came running with his rifle. "About damn time, pard. I was commencing to worry." He cocked his head. "You and that horse of yours look awful peaked. And did it rain where you were?"

"I could use some coffee." Fargo's buckskins were still damp and uncomfortable in the growing chill of the high-country night.

Cecelia had his cup full and held it out to him. "Here you go," she said as he dismounted.

"Where have you been, my good man?" Wendolyn asked. He was holding his teacup and saucer and was as impeccably dressed as ever in a hunting outfit that included a wide-brimmed hat with a high crown that he had told them was popular with big-game hunters in Africa.

Fargo hunkered by the fire for the warmth. He swallowed half the cup before he launched into a recital of his day. They listened with intense interest. No one interrupted. When he was done he drained the rest of the cup and promptly refilled it.

"So the two bears are sticking close to one another?" Rooster said thoughtfully. "Maybe the smaller one is her cub."

"Too old," Fargo said. Cubs stayed with their mothers for a year or so, two years at the most. The smaller grizzly looked to be twice that.

"Now and then a cub doesn't want to go off on its own no matter what."

"Then where this Brain Eater goes, the smaller one follows," Wendy said.

"You know what this means, don't you?" Cecelia said.

Moose, who hadn't uttered a word since Fargo arrived, roused and said, "What?"

"We have to kill both of them."

"There's no bounty on the smaller griz," Rooster said.

"So what?" Cecelia countered. "It's killed people, the same as the big one. And it will go on killin' unless it's stopped."

"I daresay I have no objection," Wendy said. "Two bears are twice the sport and twice the fun."

"Fun?" Rooster said, and snorted.

"We can always sell the hide for money," Moose said. "It won't be a lot split five ways but it will put a little extra in our pokes."

"A fine notion," Cecelia said, smiling warmly at him.

Then she turned to Fargo. "How about you, Skye? What do you say?"

"We kill both."

"This hunt is getting complicated," Rooster groused. "Killing the big one will be hard enough."

Cecelia asked Bethany to get her a clean plate and ladled

squirrel meat onto it. She added a slice of bread and handed it to Fargo, saying, "Here you go. You must be awful hungry after the day you've had."

"I'm obliged." As he speared a morsel with his fork, Fargo noticed Moose staring at him.

"Back to these bears," Wendy said. "You Yanks have more experience with the brutes. How do you suggest we go about it?"

"Very carefully," Rooster said.

The next morning the men were in position by sunrise. They waited throughout the day while Cecelia cooked and her children played and made a lot of noise.

Neither grizzly showed.

That night the men and Cecelia took turns keeping watch and maintaining the fire.

Neither bear appeared.

Two more days and nights wore on their nerves. They never knew but when one or another of the man-killers would come bursting out of nowhere to rip and rend.

The next morning dawned clear and brisk. Wendy had the last watch and woke everyone.

Fargo cast off his blanket and stood. He needed coffee but first he went to the stream. Kneeling, he dipped his hands in the cold water and splashed it on his face. Usually that was enough to jar him awake. He did it several times and wiped his face with his sleeve. As he went to rise he glanced to one side.

There was a moccasin print in a strip of mud. The print had not been there the day before because he had knelt at the exact spot.

Fargo examined it. The imprint was smooth and clear; it had been made in the past hour. He placed his hand on his Colt and stared across the stream at the wall of vegetation.

Rooster came shuffling up, and grumbling. "My old bones don't take to lying on the ground as good as they used to. I should have brought extra blankets." He stopped. "What has you looking like a dog on point?"

Fargo pointed at the mud.

"Damn," Rooster said, and squatted. "He was spying on us, I bet."

Fargo nodded.

"And where there's one there are more. The question is, how many?"

"The question is, which tribe?" Fargo said. Given where they were, it could be one of two, either the Blackfeet or the Bloods. Neither were fond of whites.

Rooster knew that, too. "This ain't good. They won't like us being here."

The rest took the news uneasily except for Wendolyn.

"I say, why the long faces? These savages won't bother us, will they? Not with all the guns we have."

"Hell, English," Rooster said. "That's just it. They might attack us to get our guns."

"Or our horses," Fargo said. The Blackfeet, in particular, esteemed horse stealing highly, almost as high as counting coup on an enemy.

Wendy patted his elephant gun. "If they try they will regret it."

"Ever fought Indians?" Rooster asked.

"I can't say as I have, no."

"Then don't act like you know what you're talking about. At short range their bows are as lethal as that cannon of yours. And they can loose arrows a damn sight faster than you can shoot."

"I still say they'll think twice. And if they attack we'll give them bloody hell."

Cecelia had her arms around her kids. "What about us? You men they'll kill and scalp. But what do they do to women and children? Take them captive?"

"The kids they might," Rooster said, and let it go at that.

"Oh," Cecelia said.

"I won't let them hurt you," Moose said. "I'll pick them up and break them over my knee like I done to a Sioux once."

"As if we didn't have enough to worry about with the bears," Rooster muttered.

Fargo was sipping coffee. "I could try to talk to them. Find out what they're up to."

"How would you go about it?" Cecelia asked.

"By going off into the woods alone. If they're still around, they might show themselves."

"Or they could stick arrows in you from ambush and put your hair on display in a lodge," Rooster said.

"I'd rather you didn't," Cecelia said. "It's too dangerous."

Moose scowled. "If he wants to we should let him. Why are you worrying about him, anyhow?"

"He's one of us," Cecelia said.

"Well, you shouldn't so much. Your kids and me are who you should worry about."

"What are you goin' on about? Naturally I worry about you and my kids."

"I'm just saying," Moose said.

"Well, you're bein' silly. We can't afford to lose Skye, not when we still have Brain Eater to kill."

"Don't forget that other bear," Rooster said.

Wendy grinned and patted his rifle. "Bears *and* savages. I must say, this is more exciting than I dared hope it would be."

Rooster squinted at him. "Tell me something, hoss."

"Anything, my fine friend."

"Are all Brits as loco as you?"

14

The forest was quiet save for the distant screech of a jay. Fargo glided from cover to cover, his ears pricked, his eyes darting from shadow to shadow.

Only a fool took the Blackfeet or their allies, the Bloods, lightly, and Fargo wasn't a fool. They were fierce fighters.

He suspected they were somewhere near, spying on him and the others, which was why he had crawled from the back of the lean-to to the stream and quickly waded across into the woods while the others stayed at the fire to try and draw attention.

Something moved up ahead. Fargo crouched and brought the Sharps to his shoulder. A doe appeared, followed by a fawn with spots, and he lowered it again.

Fargo hoped to God he could avert bloodshed. He harbored no animosity toward the Blackfeet or Bloods, or any other tribe, for that matter. He'd as soon get along with all of them. But he was white and some tribes hated whites for the same reason some whites hated Indians: the color of their skin. It was a stupid reason to hate, but if there was one thing as common as air, it was stupidity.

Fargo frowned. He was letting himself be distracted. Moving on, he crept past a high pine and several oaks. Beyond rose a low knoll. He was about to climb it when he heard a thud from the other side.

Flattening, Fargo levered on his elbows and knees to the top. He removed his hat before he peeked over.

Three horses had been tied so they couldn't wander off. None had saddles. Instead of leather bridles they had rope hackamores. On the hindquarters of one was the painted symbol of a knife.

That there were only three warriors was a mild relief. Three was better than twenty. Fargo scanned the woods but they weren't anywhere near. Jamming his hat on, he slid back down and worked around to where he could see if anyone approached.

He lay on his belly in the high grass. He figured it would be a while before they showed but it was less than five minutes later that a warrior came out of the woods. He took a few steps and abruptly stopped.

The warrior tilted his head from side to side as if he sensed or suspected that something wasn't quite right. He was armed with a lance. His features, his hair, his leggings and moccasins were those of the Blackfeet.

Fargo stayed still. Two of the horses were dozing. The third had raised its head and was staring at the warrior, its tail lazily swishing.

The Blackfoot slowly advanced. He scoured the knoll and the woods. He came to the horse nearest Fargo and reached for the hackamore.

Three swift bounds and Fargo had the Sharps' muzzle pressed hard against the nape of the man's neck. The warrior heard him and started to turn but Fargo was too quick for him. "Not so much as twitch," he warned in English. In the man's own tongue he said, "Not move." He was a lot more fluent in the Lakota language and a few others but he knew enough Blackfoot to get by.

The warrior was surprisingly calm. He stayed still as Fargo sidled around and took a few steps back.

"Do you speak the white tongue?"

The warrior stared. He was in his middle years, thirty to forty, his eyes dark and penetrating.

"Do you speak the white tongue?" Fargo asked again.

"Little some," the warrior said.

"Drop the lance," Fargo directed, and motioned with the Sharps. The warrior let it fall.

"Back away from the horse."

Again the warrior complied.

"Why are you and your friends spying on me and my friends?" Fargo asked.

"What be spying?"

"Watching us," Fargo said.

The warrior grunted.

"We have come in peace to your country," Fargo said. "We are not your enemy."

"Many guns."

"All whites carry guns," Fargo exaggerated. "Just as all warriors have a bow or a tomahawk or some other weapon. If we were here to make war we wouldn't have brought the woman and her children."

"Why come?" the warrior said, still with that surprising calm.

Fargo was about to explain when swift steps pattered behind him. He whirled but he was too late. The other two warriors were on him. He had no time to shoot. A shoulder caught him in the gut and he was lifted off his feet and slammed to the ground. Iron hands clamped on each wrist and the rifle was torn from his grasp. Bucking, he drove a knee into the back of the warrior on his right and the man cried out and his grip loosened. Fargo pulled free, twisted, and delivered an uppercut to the chin of the other. Heaving up, Fargo gained room to move. He swooped his hand to his Colt but he had forgotten about the first warrior. A blow to his back pitched him flat on his face and filled him with excruciating pain.

Fargo rolled, or tried to. The warrior was on top of him, seeking to pin his arms. With a powerful wrench Fargo made it to his knees. Pivoting, he flicked a right cross and a left jab.

Blackfeet weren't accustomed to fisticuffs. The warrior was more startled than hurt and fell back with an expression of surprise.

Again Fargo clawed for his revolver. He almost had it out when the other two pounced. An arm clamped around his throat from behind and a knee gouged his spine. The other warrior grabbed hold of his wrist to keep him from raising the Colt any higher. Fargo tensed to throw them off.

Suddenly the first warrior was in front of him, holding a knife. The warrior pressed the tip to Fargo's throat and said simply, "Stop."

Fargo stopped.

"Let go little gun."

Fargo raised his hand from the Colt. He considered himself as good as dead. He was girding to lunge at the one holding the knife when the warrior drew the blade away from his throat.

"How you called?"

"To the Lakota I am He Who Follows Many Trails," Fargo said. "To the whites I am Fargo. Who are you?"

"Bird Rattler."

Fargo recollected hearing the name before. "You are an important man in the councils of your people." Which was as high a praise as a warrior could get.

"Why you here, white man?"

Fargo saw no reason to lie. "We are on a hunt."

"For elk?"

"For bear," Fargo said. "We are after a man-killer. The whites call her Brain Eater. She likes to bite open heads and eat out the brains."

Bird Rattler lowered his knife all the way. He said something in his own tongue to the other two, too fast for Fargo to follow, and they let go of him and looked at him with interest.

"How you know bear she?"

"I've seen her," Fargo said. "Her and another bear that is following her around."

"*Kiaayo kitsiakkomimm*," Bird Rattler said.

"The other bear is her lover?" Fargo translated. It made sense. Normally, male and female grizzlies had little to do with one another. But for about four months each year, April through July, the males sought the females out to mate. If the female was in heat, a male might linger in her vicinity for weeks.

Bird Rattler grunted. "We call female"—he paused as if trying to find the right white word—"Breaks Heads. We call male Little Penis."

Fargo laughed. Then it hit him what the other was saying. "She's attacked your people too?"

"Yes."

Fargo could have slapped himself. It had never occurred to him—and it should have—that if the grizzly was attacking whites, it must also be attacking Indians. "How many has she killed?"

Bird Rattler slid his knife into his beaded sheath. He held up all the fingers and thumb on one hand and four fingers on the others.

"Nine?" Fargo said. "Damn. White and red together puts her tally at over twenty that we know of." Another insight dawned. "Are you after her too?"

Bird Rattler grunted. "Me," he said, and pointed at the other two in turn. "Red Mink. Lazy Husband. Others afraid. Say Breaks Heads bad medicine."

"She sure as hell is," Fargo agreed, and was struck by an inspiration. "I have an idea. How about if we join forces?"

"Forces?" Bird Rattler said.

"You're after her. We're after her. Why not work together and increase our chances?"

"You white," Bird Rattler said. "White men not like red man."

"Not all are that way. I'm not."

"Me must talk," Bird Rattler said, and led his companions out of earshot.

Fargo brushed himself off. His gut was sore but otherwise he was unhurt. He stared toward the Sharps. None of the warriors objected when he picked it up although Red Mink watched his every move.

The Blackfeet were arguing. Red Mink gestured sharply and Bird Rattler looked at Fargo and used a hand sign that signified, "No."

Fargo was sure the Blackfeet would have killed him if the subject of the bear hadn't come up. Lone whites who ventured into their territory were often never heard from again. He held the Sharps in the crook of his elbow as he normally would, and curled his thumb around the hammer, just in case.

The dispute ended. The three warriors came back. Red Mink didn't appear happy.

Bird Rattler, though, placed his hand on Fargo's shoulder and looked Fargo in the eye. "We help you, other whites not try kill us?"

"They do and they'll answer to me," Fargo promised.

"When kill Breaks Heads, who have hide?"

"You can keep it if it's you who kills it," Fargo said. "But the whites will need to show it down in town first. Then you can have it."

"Deal," Bird Rattler said, and held out his hand, white-fashion.

Fargo smiled and shook. "With us working together we have a good chance at killing her."

"Maybe she kill us," Bird Rattler said.

15

When Fargo rode out of the trees with the Blackfeet behind him, Cecelia was the first to spot them. She let out a holler and Rooster, Moose and Wendolyn grabbed their rifles and came on the run, Rooster going so far as to take aim and cock his Sharps.

"No!" Fargo commanded, drawing rein.

"What the hell? Those are Blackfeet, hoss."

"You think I don't know that?"

Cecelia had her own rifle and was by the lean-to, her fear-struck brood peeking past her dress. "Are there more of the savages? Do they plan to take us captive? I'll be damned if they'll lay a finger on me."

"Simmer down, both of you," Fargo said. "They're after Brain Eater, the same as us."

"The devil you say?" Wendy said. "I've heard a lot about these blighters. Can we trust them?"

"In this we can."

"Like hell," Rooster said. "I lost two good friends to the Blackfeet. I don't trust them any further than I can throw a buffalo."

"They can be of help," Fargo insisted. He turned to Moose, who was being unusually quiet again. "What do you say?"

"I say whatever Cecelia says."

All of them looked at her.

"Well?" Fargo prompted.

Cecelia regarded the Blackfeet as she might three rattlesnakes about to bite her. "You really reckon it would be safe?"

"I do," Fargo said. "And remember, they have more at stake than we do."

"How so?"

"Most of us are in it for the money," Fargo said. "They're in it to protect their people."

"They have no interest in the bounty?"

"None," Fargo confirmed.

Cecelia pursed her lips. "In that case they're welcome to stay. But only so long as they abide by my conditions."

"Which are?"

"They do what we say when we say it. They cook for themselves. They're not to go near my kids, ever. And at night they don't sleep in the lean-to. Tell them."

"No," Fargo said.

"Why in blazes not?"

"Where to begin?" Fargo responded, half to himself. "They're Blackfeet warriors. We can't tell them what to do. We can ask but whether they do it or not is up to them. They're here after Brain Eater, not your kids. They like sleeping under the stars so I doubt they'd want to sleep in the lean-to. And since they're helping us, we share our food."

"Sounds to me like you're treatin' them the same as you treat us."

"Smart gal."

"But they're *heathens*."

Fargo had met so many whites who had the same attitude that he supposed he shouldn't be disappointed, but he was. "They're people."

"Pard, that is the stupidest thing you ever said," Rooster spat.

"I say," Wendolyn interjected. "All this arguing isn't doing us any good. We need to work together."

"I'll work with anyone but the Blackfeet," Rooster declared.

"Damn it, Rooster," Fargo said.

"I'm sorry, pard. If they were Shoshones or Crows, I wouldn't mind. You can call it wrong but I can't help being me."

"Will you at least not shoot them if we let them lend us a hand?"

Rooster glared at the three warriors, who were still on their horses. "I reckon I can live and let live just this once. But only for you, you hear? Were it up to me they'd be dead already."

"Cecelia?"

"If you vouch for them I'll go along with it too," she said with obvious reluctance. "But understand me. They do anythin' I don't like, anythin' at all, they'll be gone or they'll be dead."

Fargo sighed and walked over to the Blackfeet. "You heard?"

"Me hear," Bird Rattler said.

"There's a lot of hate going around," Fargo said. "On both sides."

Bird Rattler ran a hand over his mount's mane. "When I young, I think hate good. More winters I live, not like hate so much."

"Stay away from the old one," Fargo advised. "He hates the most."

"It not old man worry me," Bird Rattler said. "It bear."

The tension was thick enough to cut with a blunt knife.

Bird Rattler and his companions made camp near the stream. By coincidence it was at the spot where Fargo and his companions usually took their horses to drink. That afternoon, Rooster took them to a different spot.

In the evening Fargo called them all together. The whites sat on one side of the fire, the Blackfeet on the other.

"If we are going to make this work," Fargo began, "we need a plan." He explained to Bird Rattler that they had hoped to lure the she-bear in close enough to shoot but so far she had only come once, and at night, and they didn't get the chance. He also mentioned that the male bear had been with her.

"Bears much hard kill."

"What was your plan?" Fargo asked him.

"Find tracks. Follow tracks. Find bear. Kill bear."

"Except bears don't always leave tracks, do they, redskin?" Rooster said sarcastically.

"No, white skin," Bird Rattler said. "They not."

"Using ourselves as bait hasn't worked either," Fargo said. "We need something better."

"Like what?" Rooster said. "Bears think with their stomachs. All they care about is food. If our horses and us ain't enough, what else can we use?"

"How about a deer?" Moose said. "We can kill one and rig it over the fire. Maybe the smell of roast meat will bring Brain Eater in again."

Fargo had a thought. "We can go that one better. We'll shoot a deer and bring it here to bleed out."

"What'll that do?"

Rooster grinned and snapped his fingers. "I get it, hoss. It's the blood. Grizzlies can smell blood from a mile off."

"They can?" Cecelia said. "Then why not kill two deer and bleed them? Or even three?"

"What do we do with all that meat?"

"Leave what we don't eat to rot."

"No, we dry it and smoke it for jerky," Fargo proposed.

Between the blood and the venison, he reckoned it just might work.

Rooster excitedly rubbed his hands together. "This is the best idea we've had yet. Let's get to it at first light."

With the rising of the sun they split into hunting parties. Bird Rattle and his friends went off in one direction, Moose and Wendy in another, Fargo and Rooster yet a third. Usually they saw a lot of deer but by midmorning they hadn't seen one. When Rooster drew rein in disgust, so did Fargo.

"Figures," the old scout complained. "There's never a deer around when you want to shoot one."

Fargo was about to say that the others might be having better luck when he spied gray coils winding skyward over a mile away and half a mile lower down. "Smoke."

"Got to be whites. Redskins are smart enough not to let folks know where they are. Should we have a look-see?"

The smoke was thinning by the time they crossed a ridge that overlooked a picturesque valley.

"Yonder, near those trees," Rooster said, pointing. He rose in his stirrups. "Do you see what I see?"

Fargo did. Shucking the Sharps from his saddle scabbard, he gigged the Ovaro. They descended through heavy timber to the valley floor.

The Ovaro nickered.

"Side by side," Fargo instructed. "You cover left, I'll cover right."

"I'll watch our backs too." Rooster's horse shied and he had to calm it.

The valley was as quiet as a cemetery. Other than a butterfly there was no sign of life. A strong breeze rustled the grass.

"It can't have been long ago if the fire's still going," Rooster said.

"No," Fargo agreed.

"The damn thing could be anywhere."

A patch of grass seemed to bulge and Fargo jerked his Sharps up. But it was only another gust.

"You're twitchy, pard," Rooster said, and chuckled.

"I'm fond of breathing," Fargo said. The smell of the smoke was strong. So was another smell that was becoming all too familiar.

The fire was down to charred wood and glowing embers. Beside it lay a coffeepot on its side and an overturned frying pan. Packs had been torn open and the contents strewn about. A sack of flour had burst, spraying flour over what was left of a man who lay sprawled facedown. His clothes were in shreds but enough remained to show he had been wearing overalls with suspenders.

"It's one of those would-be bear hunters," Rooster said. "I can't recollect his name but he makes his living as a store clerk."

Part of the clerk's head was missing. Gore oozed from the empty skull.

"Brain Eater," Rooster said.

Fargo thought he was referring to the dead man's head.

Then a gigantic shape lumbered out of the woods and growled.

16

"Shoot her!" Rooster cried, snapping his Sharps to his shoulder.

"No!" Fargo said. "Not yet!" He hoped the grizzly would rise onto her rear legs and give them a better shot at her vitals.

Rooster didn't heed. His rifle boomed. Blood sprayed from the she-bear's head and she recoiled. But the slug had only grazed her. Opening her maw, she let out with a tremendous roar.

"Ride!" Fargo bawled.

Rooster hauled on his reins but his horse had only begun to turn when Brain Eater slammed into it with the impact of an avalanche. The horse squealed and crashed down. Rooster tried to shove clear but his leg was pinned. He pushed at the saddle as his horse, kicking wildly, sought to rise.

Fargo raised his rifle. He didn't have much of a shot; the grizzly's flank was to him.

Brain Eater sank her teeth in the horse's neck. The horse shrieked, and there was a *crunch*. With a powerful wrench Brain Eater tore the stricken animal's throat out and swallowed a chunk of flesh.

Rooster was still frantically trying to free himself.

"Lie still!" Fargo shouted. The bear might ignore him if Rooster pretended to be dead.

Instead, Rooster groped in his pocket. He found a new cartridge and fumbled at inserting it. He wasn't looking at the grizzly.

Fargo fired just as Brain Eater's mouth closed on Rooster's head. Rooster screamed and tried to pull away. His eyes fixed on Fargo in terrified appeal, and then there was another, louder, *crunch* as Brain Eater ripped the top of his head off.

Transfixed, Fargo saw the grizzly stick her snout into the hole in Rooster's head, and slurp. Rooster's brain oozed out and she gobbled it down in quick gulps. Then she stepped back and turned—toward the Ovaro.

Self-preservation broke Fargo's spell. Rooster was gone and if he stayed and made a fight of it, he was as good as gone, too.

Brain Eater exploded into motion.

Fargo fled. The stallion galloped toward the far end of the valley with the giant grizzly pounding in pursuit. Teeth gnashed; the bear was biting at the Ovaro's tail. Fargo twisted and fired at the grizzly's broad skull. He hit it, too, because a scarlet furrow blossomed. His slug, like Rooster's, failed to penetrate.

But Brain Eater did slow and shake her head as if she were trying to clear it.

Fargo galloped on. When he glanced over his shoulder the grizzly had stopped. He didn't. Not until he was in the trees.

Brain Eater was tearing at the dead horse. She ignored Rooster. Apparently the only part of a human she liked to eat were the brains.

Fargo stared at his friend, thinking of former times. "Damn." Yet another he had lost. At the rate things were going, by the time he reached old age he wouldn't have any friends left.

He had a decision to make. He could tuck tail and ride off, leaving the grizzly free to go on killing, or he could try to stop the slaughter once and for all.

Dismounting, Fargo tied off the reins. He could get closer on foot than on horseback. He reloaded and stalked along the tree line toward the bear. She was so intent on her feast, she'd forgotten about him.

Fargo moved from cover to cover with the speed of molasses. Any faster, and the movement might give him away.

Brain Eater was standing side-on. Fargo had a good shot if he could get close enough.

The grizzly gnawed at an eye socket. She seemed to like eyes as much as she liked brains.

Fargo raised his Sharps but didn't shoot. Not yet. He needed to be certain. He skirted a small blue spruce and stopped dead.

Brain Eater was staring in his direction.

Fargo broke out in a sweat. Had she or hadn't she seen him? He was too far from the Ovaro to reach it if she came after him.

Brain Eater resumed feeding. But something in the way she stood warned Fargo that she was suspicious and was keeping her eye on his vicinity. He took a step and she raised her head.

Fargo froze.

The grizzly raised her muzzle and sniffed. Shifting, she resumed filling her stomach.

Fargo flattened. She couldn't see him now so it was safe to move faster. Or so he thought until he heard a growl and raised his head high enough to see over the grass.

Brain Eater had stopped feeding and was holding her head high, scenting the wind. Blood dribbled from her mouth and gleamed red on her throat.

Fargo crabbed to an oak. Keeping it between him and the bear, he slowly stood and brought the Sharps to his shoulder. He was close enough.

Brain Eater was still testing the breeze.

I've got you now, Fargo thought. He aligned the front sight with the rear sight and placed his finger on the trigger.

All he had to do was cock the hammer.

Another growl sent a ripple of consternation down Fargo's spine. It didn't come from in front of him. It came from *behind* him. He took his cheek from the Sharps and looked over his shoulder.

It was the other bear, the male, the one the Blackfeet called Little Penis.

Even as Fargo set eyes on him, Little Penis charged.

Fargo had no time to shoot and nowhere to run. Instead he jumped at a low limb, caught hold, and pulled himself into the tree. He barely made it. Claws raked his boot. He scrambled higher. The male reared and bit at Fargo's leg, and missed.

Fargo gained a new hold, rising out of reach. Little Penis didn't like that. He roared and clawed at the oak and might have gone on clawing at it if not for crashing in the brush.

Suddenly Brain Eater was there.

The grizzlies stared at one another and Little Penis sank onto all fours.

Fargo tried to aim at her but branches were in the way. He carefully shifted to find a better position.

Brain Eater came to the tree. She looked up, tilting her head to see him. She sniffed the air and the male sniffed her and she turned to him and they rubbed heads.

Fargo still didn't have a shot.

Brain Eater uttered a low whine and moved off into the timber. Little Penis went on sniffing, and followed.

Fargo waited several minutes after the sounds of their passage faded before he risked descending. Bears sometimes circled back on prey, although in this instance he suspected they had something else on their minds.

Once he was on the ground, Fargo ran. He was covered with sweat and puffing when he climbed on the Ovaro. The smart thing to do was leave, to get as far from the two grizzlies as he could. Instead he rode down the valley to Rooster.

Fargo scanned the slopes above. He didn't expect to see the bears but he did. They were climbing side by side. As he watched, they stopped and rubbed against one another and then moved into a dense growth of firs.

"True love," Fargo said, but he didn't laugh. Climbing down, he went through Rooster's pockets, then dragged the body into the shade and covered the old scout's remains with branches and rocks and dirt. He also salvaged what he could from Rooster's saddlebags. He tied Rooster's Sharps on the Ovaro with his bedroll.

A dry blood trail led him to the man who made the fire: another bear hunter. The man had lost an arm and a foot and half his head was gone. So was his brain.

The sun was on its westward incline when Fargo reined the Ovaro to the northwest. He wasn't going after the two grizzlies alone. One, yes, he could handle, but to tackle two was to ask for an early grave.

Twilight was spreading its colorless blanket over the wilds when Fargo reached the meadow. The others were already back.

Moose and Wendy were by the fire with Cecelia and the kids. The Blackfeet were at their own fire near the stream. He wearily climbed down. Without saying a word he knelt and helped himself to coffee and gulped half the cup.

Everyone stared. The Blackfeet came over and waited for him to say something.

It was Moose who glanced into the woods and said, "Where's Rooster? Did you leave the old goat behind?"

"He's dead," Fargo said.

"I'm sorry," Cecelia said. "I know him and you go a ways back."

"Breaks Heads?" Bird Rattler asked.

Fargo nodded. "She and the male are together."

"As if the one ain't problem enough," Cecelia said.

Moose nodded. "They could stay together for days or weeks. It'll be that much harder for us."

"Twice the challenge, eh, mates?" Wendy said with a happy grin.

Fargo was refilling his cup. "Rooster wouldn't think so."

"What do we do?" Cecelia asked. "How do we kill two bears when we can't kill the one?"

All eyes fixed on Fargo again. "Could be they'll lay up for a while," he guessed. "They have Rooster's horse to eat so they won't be in a hurry to go anywhere. We can go back there tomorrow and end this."

"All of us?" Moose said, and shook his head. "I'm staying with Cecelia."

"No," she said.

"I won't leave you and the kids alone."

"You don't take part, we're not entitled to any of the bounty."

Fargo spoke up. "You each get your share whether he comes or not. It will be safer for you if he stays."

"I won't be coddled," Cecelia said.

"I'd be too worried," Moose said.

"What can happen? The bears are miles from here." Cecelia looked at Bird Rattler. "Are there any other of your people hereabouts?"

"No."

"There you have it," Cecelia said to Moose. "We'll be perfectly fine. You go off with these others and do what you have to."

"But—" Moose began, and she held up a hand.

"I won't have a man who uses me as an excuse."

"It's not—" Moose started again, but this time she covered his mouth with her palm.

"Prove to me you're worth a damn. Go off and help kill Brain Eater and that other one if you have to and get us the money we need." She removed her hand. "You hear me?"

94

"Whatever you say," Moose said.

"That's settled then." Cecelia smiled sweetly. "It's getting late. I'd better start on supper." She collected her kids and ushered them toward the lean-to.

"You know," Wendy said, "I've hunted elephant and rhino. I've pitted myself against tigers and jaguars. But there's nothing on this earth half as formidable as a woman with her dander up."

"Does that mean you'd be scared of her if you was me?" Moose asked.

"In a word, my good man, yes."

Moose sighed. "I sure could use a drink right about now."

"We all could," Fargo said.

17

Buzzards covered the horse. They tore at the flesh with their beaks and swallowed the meat whole. A red fox sat on its haunches nearby. Twice it had approached but the vultures hissed and flapped their wings and the fox timidly retreated.

"I don't see no bears," Moose said.

They were on the ridge Fargo had crossed the day before. Sunlight bathed the valley. Only the thickest of the timber was in shadow. A yellow finch was conspicuous. So was a jay high in a pine.

"Where did you see the fearsome blighters last?" Wendy asked.

Fargo pointed at the firs on the opposite slope. "Going into those trees."

"They might still be there," Moose said.

"You're the expert on bears," Wendolyn said. "Do we wait for them to come out or do we go in after them?"

Bird Rattler and his friends had not uttered a word the entire ride. But now the venerable warrior cleared his throat and said, "Go in."

"Catch them napping, as it were?" Wendy said. "I like the idea."

Fargo didn't. Something was bothering him but he couldn't put his mental finger on the cause.

"Piikani go there," Bird Rattler said, and pointed at the west end of the fir belt. "White-eyes go there," and he pointed at the east end.

"Piikani?" Wendy said.

"It's what the Blackfeet call themselves," Fargo explained. The names that whites called most tribes weren't their real names. The Apaches were the Shis-Inday. The Comanches called themselves the Numunu. The Crows were the Apsaalooke.

"It'll take us half the day to get up there," Moose observed.

"Stay here if you want," Wendy said. "Personally, I like going into the bush after dangerous game. It adds to the thrill."

"I didn't say I wouldn't go."

Wendy ran a hand over his elephant gun. "At last I can put my beauty to the test."

They agreed that each group would start into the firs when the sun was at its zenith. Then they separated and began their climb. The terrain was rugged, their ascent arduous. Still, Fargo and his companions reached the fir belt half an hour before they were to move in. "We'll rest a bit," he announced. Shucking the Sharps, he sat with his back to a boulder, plucked a blade of grass, and stuck it in his mouth. From where he sat he could see the buzzards and the fox.

Wendy breathed deep of the rarefied air, and smiled.

"I daresay I like this country of yours. These mountains stir the very soul."

"They're just mountains," Moose said.

"That's like saying the ocean is just water. Look about you." The Brit gestured. "These noble crags and lofty heights are a testament to the grandeur of creation. They would inspire a poet to rapturous verse."

"Raptu-what?"

"The hand of an artist is everywhere. Don't you feel it?"

"I don't know what in hell you're talking about," Moose said.

The Britisher appealed to Fargo. "Surely you understand. Explain it to him, if you would."

"I don't need him to," Moose said. "I ain't dumb. You got your head in the clouds."

"I doubt you comprehend at all," Wendy said.

Moose bunched his fists. "Keep talking to me like that and so help me, I'll pound you."

"Talk a little louder so the bloody bears will know we're here."

"They already do."

"Is that true?" Wendy asked Fargo.

"Odds are," Fargo said.

"Then how do we sneak up on them?"

"We don't."

97

"Is this like tiger hunting? Do we go in and make a lot of noise and drive them toward the Indians? Or do the Indians drive them toward us?"

"Drive a grizzly?" Moose said, and laughed.

"We go in and hope we get off a shot before they claw us to bits," Fargo said.

"You make it sound as if we're depending entirely on luck."

"Now the foreigner gets it," Moose said.

Wendolyn muttered something about Yanks, shouldered his elephant gun, and walked away.

Moose chuckled. "I reckon I hurt his feelings."

"Go easy on him. That elephant gun of his could come in handy."

"That reminds me," Moose said. "I'm been meaning to ask. What the blazes is an elephant, anyhow?"

Fargo had been keeping an eye on the sun, and now he stood. "I'll tell you later. It's time to start in."

"Look out, Brain Eater," Moose said. "Here we come."

Firs grew high and straight and thin. They were so closely spaced that their trunks were in perpetual shadow. Fargo and the others had to thread through a maze of narrow gaps, often with limbs practically poking them in the face.

Of all the places the two grizzlies could pick to lie low, this was especially dangerous. The bears could charge out of anywhere at any time.

Fargo held the Sharps in his left hand with the stock on his leg and the barrel against his chest where it was less apt to be snared by limbs. Moose was thirty feet or so to this right, Wendy about the same distance to his left. So far they had penetrated over a hundred yards and the only sign of life had been a few birds and a chipmunk that chattered and scampered off.

Fargo probed the shadowed gloom. A mistake could cost them their lives. His nerves were on edge. When a finch took startled wing, he gave a slight start himself.

Skirting several tightly clustered boles, Fargo drew rein.

On the ground were droppings. That they were bear was obvious.

That they were left the day before would be easy to confirm

but he didn't climb down and risk being pounced on. He clucked to the stallion.

The minutes crawled. It was half a mile to the middle of the stand. The heat and the quiet took a toll. Drowsiness nipped at him but he shook it off.

They spooked a rabbit. They sent a doe and two fawns bounding off. A cow elk snorted and plunged away through the undergrowth in a panic.

Fargo had not seen bear sign since the droppings but now he came on a tree with claw marks and another where the bark had been rubbed off and crinkly hairs stuck to it.

Wendy drew rein and extended an arm.

Fargo looked but didn't see anything. He thought it must be the Brit's imagination. Then a large shape detached from a mass of shadow. Snapping the Sharps up, he was about to shoot when the shape stepped into a sunbeam. "Another damn elk," he said in disgust.

The firs seemed unending. With the sun screened by the tall trees, Fargo had to guess how much time had passed. About an hour, more or less, he reckoned, when the Ovaro pricked its ears.

Ahead, something moved.

Fargo brought the Sharps up again but snapped it down. He stopped and waited for the approaching rider to reach him. "Any sign?"

"No," Bird Rattler said. "You see bears?"

Fargo shook his head.

"They not here," the warrior stated the obvious, sounding as disappointed as Fargo felt.

Red Mink and Lazy Husband converged from either side. Moose and Wendy joined them, and the looks on all their faces said all there was to say.

Fargo reined down the mountain. It would take them until long past dark to reach the meadow. Were it not for Cecelia and her children, he'd make camp in this valley and head back to them in the morning.

The buzzards were gluttons. They had eaten down to the skeleton and half a dozen were up to their feathered bellies in intestines and organs. The stink was abominable.

Fargo gave them a wide berth. The feeling that had pricked

at him all day came over him stronger than ever. He stopped and stared at the ungainly birds and racked his head for a reason.

"What's the matter?" Moose asked. "I want to get back to Cecelia quick as we can."

"Something's not right," Fargo said.

"About those beastly scavengers?" Wendy said, viewing the vultures with distaste. "They're ugly blokes, I'll grant you, but they serve a purpose. I've seen their like on every continent."

"Not them," Fargo said. "Something else."

"Can you be more specific?"

"I wish to hell I could." Fargo watched a buzzard tug at a strip of flesh that was stuck to a leg bone.

"Let's keep going," Moose urged. "It'll be dark soon and Cecelia and her little ones are alone."

"You act like their father," Wendy teased.

"Maybe I will be," Moose said. "Cecelia is looking for a new husband. I might not be much of a catch but she says I can be trained."

Wendy laughed. "Ah, yes. Don't you find it ironic that women marry a man and then want to change him into something he wasn't when they said 'I do'?"

Moose shrugged. "I don't mind changing some if I get to be in the same bed with her every night."

"Sex," Wendy said. "The great equalizer."

"God, you talk peculiar. And you better not be thinking of Cecelia when you say that word."

"Perish forbid," Wendy said.

Moose motioned impatiently at Fargo. "What are we waiting for? Those bears ain't anywhere near here."

"No, they're not," Fargo said, and the vague notion that had been troubling him was suddenly clear as crystal. "Son of a bitch," he blurted.

"What's wrong?" Moose asked.

"Why didn't I see it sooner?"

"See what?"

"Brain Eater never came back to her kill."

Moose looked as confused as a human being could be. "So she didn't come back? What difference does that make?"

"A grizzly wouldn't let that much meat go to waste unless it had a damn good reason."

"She wasn't hungry or she was busy with the male," Moose said. "When bears mate they don't think about food as much. I'm like that myself but after it's over I'm always hungry as can be."

"Brain Eater didn't finish the horse because she wasn't here," Fargo said, "and if she wasn't here, where was she?"

"I still don't savvy."

Fargo raised his reins. "Ride," he said. "Ride like the wind and hope to God I'm wrong."

18

A full moon cast the meadow in pale light. They came out of the trees and drew rein, their exhausted horses hanging their heads.

Wendy cleared his throat. "I say, the fire has gone out. Weren't they supposed to keep it going night and day?"

"Cecelia!" Moose hollered, and used his heels with no thought to his own safety.

"Damn," Fargo said. He went after him. He still hoped he was wrong but the Brit had a point; the fire should still be burning. Fire was one of the few things most bears were afraid of. Cecelia knew that. And with her children at stake, she wouldn't let it go out.

Moose frantically bellowed her name. He was the first to reach the camp. Drawing rein, he exclaimed, "My God! The lean-to!"

Fargo was off the Ovaro before it stopped moving. The structure was a shambles, the limbs and brush in bits and pieces. So were many of the articles that had been in it.

"No, no, no, no," Moose said, moving amid the ruin in a daze.

"Fargo!" Wendy called. "Over here." He was on a knee by the charred vestige of their fire. "Look at this."

Partially burned logs were scattered about. A gouge in the earth explained why.

"It looks as if the ruddy bear attacked the fire," Wendy marveled.

Fargo turned to the Blackfeet. "We need your help. The woman and her children are missing."

Bird Rattler grunted and translated for his friends and the three spread out.

Fargo took only a couple of steps when fingers like iron spikes clamped onto his arm.

"Where are they?" Moose cried.

"Their horses are gone. It could be they escaped."

Moose didn't seem to hear him. His fingers dug deeper. "If anything has happened to them I won't ever forgive myself. I should never have went with you."

"We should help the others look."

"I didn't want to go," Moose said. "You heard me. I was against it but she made me."

"Moose, listen—" Fargo said, but the big bear hunter turned and ran off in erratic circles bawling Cecelia's name. Fargo went to where the horses had been. The ground was churned by their hooves. He was moving toward the stream when light flared and flames crackled. "Bring a brand," he hollered, and Wendy jogged to join him.

"Anything, mate?"

"Not yet."

"Our big friend is beside himself," Wendy said, nodding at Moose, who was at the other end of the meadow, continuing to bellow. "Can't say as I blame him. I'd be worried sick if it was my woman. Do we go off into the woods after them?"

Rubbing his beard, Fargo debated. Tracking at night was a painstaking chore. Even with torches, it took forever. Plus their horses were worn out and they weren't much better off. As much as he disliked to say it, he did. "We wait until first light."

"That's the smart thing," Wendy agreed. "But I predict you-know-who won't like it."

Moose didn't. "Why are you two standing here?" he demanded when he stopped running and shouting and came to the fire. "We have to keep looking. All night, if need be."

"No," Fargo said.

Moose had turned but stopped. "What the hell do you mean, no? Cecelia and her kids are out there somewhere and they need us."

"They could be anywhere," Fargo said. "It's no good for us to blunder around in the dark."

"We'll yell a lot. They're bound to hear us."

"So will the bears."

"No. We're doing it and I won't hear no argument."

"Use your head," Fargo said.

"I'll use something," Moose angrily retorted. Setting his rifle down, he cocked his fists.

Fargo backpedaled. A jab clipped his jaw. A straight arm brushed his shoulder. He blocked an overhand to the face. The force, though, sent him staggering. He recovered, heard Wendy holler, and Moose was on him. Knuckles the size of walnuts grazed his head and his hat went flying. Planting himself, he rammed a hard right to Moose's gut and whipped an uppercut to Moose's jaw. All Moose did was blink. Fargo dodged a clumsy hook and retaliated with a flurry that should have set Moose back on his heels. Moose absorbed the punishment like a sponge.

"Stop this fight this instant!" Wendy shouted while trying to step between them.

"Butt out!" Moose roared, and gave the Brit a shove that sent Wendy sprawling.

"Calm down!" Fargo tried, and a fist arced at his face. Ducking, he flicked a right cross. He might as well have hit solid rock.

Moose paused, his face twisted in fury. "Are you going to help hunt for her or not?"

"At daybreak."

"You can't get it through your head," Moose said. "She needs us *now*. She could be lying out there hurt, for all we know. Or worse. So you're going if I have to throw you over a saddle and tie you down."

"Use some sense."

"I'll use something else," Moose growled, and waded in anew.

Fargo's temper snapped. He'd tried to reason but Moose was too mad to listen, and Fargo would be damned if he was anyone's punching bag. As Moose sprang, he twisted and drove his right fist into the pit of Moose's stomach. Moose grunted and folded but stayed on his feet. Fargo remedied that with two swift blows to the ear that caused Moose to fall to his knees. Instantly, Fargo skipped in and swung a solid right to the chin. He almost broke his hand but Moose swayed and his eyelids fluttered and he keeled onto his side.

"You did it!" Wendy whooped.

Fargo wasn't so sure. He poked Moose a few times. The bear

hunter didn't move but he did groan. Fargo went to the Ovaro for his rope.

"Is that necessary?"

"You saw him," Fargo said. He bound Moose's wrists and was doing the same to his ankles when the night disgorged the three Blackfeet.

Bird Rattler would make a good poker player. He showed no surprise at seeing Moose on the ground. "We use big white as bait now?" he dryly asked.

"We should, the jackass," Fargo said. He had a welt on his temple and his head hurt like hell. "Any sign of the woman and her little ones?"

"We not find," Bird Rattler reported. "Come back. Wait for sun."

"I'll make coffee," Fargo volunteered. He needed sleep but the fight had his blood racing. And it wouldn't hurt to sit up a while and see if Cecelia showed.

Bird Rattler started to lead his horse off and the other two did the same.

"Where do you think you're going?" Fargo asked.

"Make our fire," the Blackfoot said.

"Like hell. From now on you sit with us and share our food."

"Maybe him not want," Bird Rattler said, indicating Moose.

"I don't give a damn. After what he just did he doesn't have a say." Fargo looked around for the coffeepot. It had been knocked a good ten feet from the fire. Retrieving it, he headed for the stream. He wasn't expecting company but he got some.

"I'd like a word," Wendolyn said.

"What's stopping you?"

"You are. You're in a bit of a snit and I can do without having my head bit off."

"So long as you don't take a swing at me we'll get along fine."

"Very well, then. The issue is this." Wendy paused. "I'm having second thoughts. We've lost your friend and now possibly Mrs. Mathers and her children. I have to ask. Is five thousand dollars worth all these lives?"

"We quit now, Rooster died for nothing. I'm seeing it through no matter what you or anyone else does."

"I didn't say I was bowing out," Wendy said quickly. "In

case you haven't heard, we British are famous for our stiff upper lips."

Fargo reached the stream and squatted to dip the pot in the water.

"I heard something," Wendy whispered. "There." He extended his elephant gun toward the other side.

All Fargo heard was the babbling of the water. He had about decided it was nothing when a plaintive cry came out of the darkness.

"Help us, please."

Fargo dropped the pot and splashed across. Three small faces peered at him from atop the bank.

"Up here, mister," Abner said.

"Hurry," Bethany begged.

"She's hurt real bad," Thomas added.

Fargo scrambled up and over and nearly stepped on Cecelia. She was on the ground, a hand pressed to her side, her skin like chalk. Her eyes were shut. "Cecelia?" he said, but got no answer.

"She passed out," Abner said. "We didn't know what to do."

"Help her," Bethany begged.

Fargo carefully moved Cecelia's hand, and grimaced.

Behind him Wendy said, "My word. I'll go heat water and cut bandages."

"The bear did it," Bethany said, her eyes brimming with tears.

"It came out of nowhere," Thomas said.

"Brain Eater?" Fargo figured.

"No," Abner answered. "It was the other one. The small bear. The male."

"It knocked Ma down and clawed her," Thomas said.

"She threw fire in its face," Bethany said.

"Stand back," Fargo directed. Easing his hands under Cecelia, he gently lifted her and carried her down the bank. She didn't stir. Her head lolled against his chest and once she groaned. The children trooped after him.

The Blackfeet made room as Fargo set Cecelia down near the fire. The bear's claws had caught her across the ribs. Bone gleamed from torn flesh. She had bled so much that her dress was stiff with dry blood.

"When did it attack you?" Fargo asked Abner as he felt for a pulse; it was pitifully weak and erratic.

"About noon," the oldest said. "Ma made soup and we were sittin' down to eat."

"We ran and hid," Thomas said. "The bear didn't come after us. It wanted the food."

"Will she live, mister?" Bethany anxiously asked.

Fargo honestly couldn't say.

19

"We're leaving and that's that," Moose announced.

The sun had been up for an hour. Fargo yawned and stretched and yearned for sleep.

Moose had behaved himself when he came to and saw that Cecelia was hurt. After Fargo untied him, the big hunter hovered over her with her hand clasped in his. The kids sat close to him and fell asleep with their heads on his leg.

About an hour before dawn Cecelia had come around. The first thing she did was ask for her children. The second was ask for water. Moose held a cup to her lips and she gratefully swallowed. She thanked him and passed out again.

Fargo leaned against his saddle and wearily rubbed his eyes. When he lowered his hand, she was staring at them.

"What was that I just heard?"

"Cecelia!" Moose beamed and bent and kissed her on the cheek. "How are you feeling? Is there anything I can get you? Anything I can do for you? Anything you need me to do for the kids?"

"You can hush," Cecelia said. Gritting her teeth, she shifted and touched the bandage. "No wonder I hurt like the dickens. That critter took a sizable chunk out of me."

Before anyone could stop her, Bethany threw herself at her mother and hugged her tight. Cecelia grimaced in pain but didn't scold her.

Sobbing, the girl said, "Oh, Ma. I was so scared. I thought you'd die."

"So did I," Moose said, earning a stern look from Cecelia. "Well, I did, and it helped me make up my mind."

"About what?"

"Us leaving," Moose said. "This is no place for you and yours. I'm taking you back to town."

"The blazes you are," Cecelia said. "I'm not givin' up my share of the bounty for you or anybody else."

"The money be damned, woman. You matter more."

Cecelia was set to voice an angry reply, but stopped. Her features softened and she said, "That's plumb sweet of you. But I'm a grown woman and can do as I please."

"You used to, you could."

"I beg your pardon?"

"We're together now. We ain't married yet but it's the same. You said so yourself. And if we're together then I have a say and my say is that I'm getting you and the kids out of these mountains."

"But the bounty . . ."

"We'll make do without it. I don't earn a lot but it's enough that we won't go without clothes on our backs or food in our bellies."

"We'd lose your share, too."

Fargo had heard enough. "Both of you get full shares whether you're here or not."

"Why would you do that for us after I whomped on you?" Moose asked.

Shrugging, Fargo looked at Cecelia and her kids. "Figure it out yourself."

"It's awful kind," Cecelia said, "but I've never shirked a job my whole life."

"You've lost a gallon of blood," Fargo recited. "Your rib is busted and the bear cut you so deep I had to stitch you with Wendy's fishing line. It'll be a week or two before you're back on your feet and you won't be yourself for a month or more. I wouldn't call that shirking."

"Listen to him," Moose said.

Cecelia tried to sit up but couldn't. "I reckon I have to give in. But not 'cause you want me to. I can't protect my young'uns, the state I'm in."

"You can't travel, either," Fargo said. "Not today, anyway."

Moose agreed to stay with her while Fargo and the rest went after the male grizzly. They headed out within the hour. Tracks on the other side of the stream pointed due north. Once in the woods the sign was scarcer but Fargo stuck to the bear's trail.

Noon came and went.

Fargo was in the lead, Wendy behind him, then Bird Rattler, Red Mink and Lazy Husband. Wooded slopes funneled them to the mouth of a gorge.

The tracks showed that the bear had gone in—but hadn't come out.

Fargo eyed the high walls and shadows. "I don't like it. It's a good spot for the bear to jump us."

"The brute probably went on out the other side," Wendy said.

"I should go on ahead while you wait here."

"Nonsense, my good fellow," the Brit disagreed. "Why should you take all the risks? We'll all go in and if you're right about the bear it will be too bloody bad for him." Wendy patted his elephant gun.

Against his better judgment Fargo gigged the Ovaro. The still air and the blazing sun turned the gorge into an oven. He was sweating profusely before they went fifty feet. Vegetation was sparse. The tracks in the dust showed that the grizzly had wandered from one side of the gorge to the other.

Wendy removed his hat and wiped his brow with a sleeve. "I say, it's deuced hot. Reminds me of the time I crossed the Sahara Desert."

"From the sounds of things, you've been most everywhere," Fargo idly remarked.

"Not really," Wendy said. "I've hunted on most every continent but there's so much I haven't set eyes on yet."

"Did you hunt a lot as a boy?"

"Hardly at all. My passion came to me later in life."

The Blackfeet had spread out and were three abreast, Bird Rattler in the center. He and Lazy Husband had arrows nocked. Red Mink held a lance.

"Is there anything you're passionate about?" Wendolyn asked. "Something you couldn't give up if you tried and you're not about to try."

"Women," Fargo said.

"I can take them or leave them. You ask me, they're more of a nuisance than they're worth. A man has to cater to their every wish. And they're so emotional. I knew a woman once who would burst into tears at the drop of a feather and she'd drop the feather."

"They have their good points."

A bend hid the next stretch.

"A female can't compare to the excitement of the kill," Wendy went on. "When I'm looking down my barrel into the eyes of a charging rhino or tiger, I'm as close as mortal man can be to ecstasy."

"If you say so." Fargo would rather attain the heights of pleasure with a woman's thighs wrapped around him.

"You don't feel a thrill when you shoot a wild beast?"

"I only do it for food or to defend myself."

They went around the bend. To the right was a thicket. To the left the stone wall had partially buckled, creating a ramp of stones and earth.

"You must have felt a tingle once or twice," Wendy persisted. "Haven't you ever been charged by a buffalo? Or a moose?"

"Both. And I could go my whole life without having it happen again."

The three warriors were talking in low tones. Something had agitated them.

"Where's your sense of adventure, man?" Wendy teased. "Where's your zest for a challenge?"

Stones clattered. Fargo glanced back just as the male grizzly rose up at the top of the ramp. Uttering a thunderous roar, it was on the Blackfeet in less time than they could blink. Red Mink was nearest and his horse bore the brunt of the impact. Both mount and warrior crashed to the ground, Red Mink thrusting with his lance as he went down. The tip sliced into the grizzly's shoulder but didn't penetrate far enough to inflict much of a wound. The bear bit down on the horse's mane and there was the *crack* of its spine breaking.

Bird Rattler let an arrow fly.

Fargo reined around and tugged on the Sharps. It was caught in the scabbard.

Red Mink made it to his knees and stabbed at the grizzly's chest. He drew the lance back to try again but the bear's claws flashed once, twice, three times, and Red Mink's head was left hanging by a ribbon of flesh. Blood pumped in a fine mist.

Bird Rattler loosed another arrow.

The Sharps came free and Fargo jammed the stock to his shoulder.

Lazy Husband was trying to control his bucking horse.

The grizzly had both front paws on Red Mink. Two feathered shafts jutted from its body but it didn't seem to feel the pain. Growling, it charged Bird Rattler, who was sighting down another arrow. Bird Rattler tried to wheel his mount but the grizzly reached it before he could break into a gallop. Flashing paws met the horse's hide and blood spurted. The horse shrieked and staggered.

Fargo fired. He didn't have a heart or lung shot so he went for the head and scored but the slug glanced off. He grabbed for another cartridge.

"God in heaven, man, move!" Wendy bellowed.

Fargo realized he was between the Brit and the griz, and reined aside.

The grizzly swung toward them. Blood flecked its maw and its front paws. Powerful muscles rippling, it barreled at the Ovaro.

An artificial thunderclap filled the gorge. The walls seemed to shake and dust rained down and the bear pitched into a slide that ended with its nose inches from the stallion's leg.

"Son of a bitch," Fargo blurted.

Wendy patted his smoking rifle. "I told you this beauty would get the job done."

The two-bore was a cannon. The slug had shattered the grizzly's skull. A hole big enough for Fargo to stick his fist in oozed gore.

"Easy as pie," Wendy boasted.

"Brain Eater won't be," Fargo predicted. "She's twice as big as this one."

"And elephants are twice as big as she is. All I need is a clear shot and I'll end her savage spree as easily as I ended the life of this one." Wendy laughed and commenced to reload. "When you've faced down as many meat-eaters of all kinds as I have, a grizzly is—what's that expression? Oh, yes. A grizzly is small potatoes."

"You wish," Fargo said.

20

Moose fixed supper. He shot a grouse and plucked it and roasted the meat on a spit.

Cecelia complained about not being allowed to help but she was too weak to sit up, let alone stand.

Bird Rattler and Lazy Husband had brought Red Mink back, swaddled in a blanket. They accepted portions of meat and then sat apart, talking.

Fargo caught snatches of what they were saying so he wasn't surprised when Bird Rattler came over and stood waiting for them to acknowledge his presence. "What is it?"

"Our friend dead."

"I am sorry for your loss," Fargo said.

"Bad medicine him die."

"We weren't careful enough."

Bird Rattler went on as if he hadn't heard. "My people say not come. Say bear much bad medicine. But I come."

"We're glad you did," Fargo tried to soothe him, "and we hope you'll stick around a good long while."

"In morning we go. Take Red Mink our people."

"You're runnin' out?" Cecelia said. "I admit I don't think highly of redskins but I never took you to have a yellow streak."

"Yellow streak?" Bird Rattler said.

"You're a scaredy-cat," Cecelia replied. "You have no more grit than mud."

"Mud?" Bird Rattler was confused.

"She says you're an old woman," Fargo made it plain. Among the Blackfeet, for a man to be called that was the insult of insults.

Bird Rattler stiffened.

113

"And you're wrong," Fargo told Cecelia. "In the fight today he stood his ground. He's as brave as any of us."

"Not if he runs off, he ain't," she said. "And if they're goin', Moose and me should rethink headin' for Gold Creek."

"No you don't," Moose said. "You're not using this as an excuse to stay."

"But it will just be Skye and the foreigner," Cecelia protested. "We owe it to them to lend a hand."

"What can you lend?" Moose said. "You can't hardly walk." He looked at Fargo. "I'm sorry. I'm taking her whether she likes it or not."

"Damn you," Cecelia said. "I don't like bein' bossed around."

"It's not my fault I care for you."

Wendy was cleaning his Holland and Holland and chose that moment to say, "Don't worry about Fargo and me, Mrs. Mathers. My elephant gun will drop Brain Eater in her tracks just as it did the male."

"I wish I'd've seen that," Cecelia said.

"It was glorious," Wendolyn said.

"You must be awful strong. That time you let me hold your rifle, it was so heavy, I could barely hold it steady to take aim."

"I'm strong, too," Moose said.

The rest of the evening passed quietly. Fargo kept to himself. Despite the Brit's confidence, Brain Eater wouldn't be easy. She was a lot bigger and a lot tougher and a lot cannier. It occurred to him that with the male dead, she might go elsewhere in search of a new mate—in which case they might not ever find her.

The sky changed from gray to purple to black. Stars in their multitude sparkled in the firmament. From out of their dens and thickets came the meat-eaters, and soon the mountains were alive with howls and yips and cries.

Fargo remembered going back east once, and how the nights were so quiet. Most of the wolves and mountain lions had been killed off. Coyotes were few and bears were fewer. He imagined that in a hundred years the same would be true of the Rockies. Cecelia turned in early, Abner, Thomas and Bethany on either side of her, Bethany with her hand in her mother's.

When the four were asleep, Moose rose and came around the fire. He sank down with a sigh and said in earnest, "I'm right sorry about running out on you."

"I understand," Fargo said.

"I've never run out on anyone. I want you to know that. But you can see how it is."

"I understand," Fargo said again.

Moose gazed at the sleeping figures. "Life sure is strange. I came here looking for a bear and found a family." He chuckled. "Me, of all people."

"Where will you go? What will you do?"

"I figure to head down Denver way. There's plenty of mountains and bears for me to hunt. There's more people, too, and the kids and Cecelia will like that. It'll be safer for them."

"She's a good woman," Fargo said.

"Smart, too. It puzzles me, a gal like her latching on to a man like me. I wouldn't ever repeat this to anyone else, but I ain't all that bright. I know it and I make the best of it, but we are what we are."

"The two of you will do fine together."

Moose held out his hand. "I don't hold a grudge over those fights we had. I respect you more than I do most. You stand up for yourself, the same as me."

Fargo shook. "I ever get down Denver way, I'll look you up."

"You do that." Moose rose. "I'm fixing to turn in, too. Wake me for the second watch." Fargo nodded.

The bear hunter spread his blanket beside his new family and was soon snoring louder than all of them combined.

Lazy Husband was asleep, too, but not Bird Rattler. He stared into the flames, his chin in his hands. "Me sorry too."

"You can't ignore bad medicine," Fargo said. He had lived with Indians. Their beliefs were as entrenched as white beliefs. He didn't always agree with either but he respected those who were sincere.

Bird Rattler looked at him. "Bad medicine for you, too."

"I can't go," Fargo said.

"Because bear kill friend?"

"Because of a lot of things," Fargo said, and smiled wryly. "But mainly because I'm too stubborn to know when to quit."

"You not quit," Bird Rattler said, "maybe you die."

By midnight fewer roars and screams and cries echoed off the high peaks. The camp lay quiet under the mantle of darkness.

Fargo put a fresh batch of coffee on. He was supposed to sit up until about one. He yawned and stretched and heard a splash in the stream. His hand dropped to the Sharps but it was only a doe. She came into the light, stared a bit, and melted away.

Fargo relaxed. The bear might be miles away. He'd start after her in the morning and this time he would stick to her trail as relentlessly as a hound to the scent of a raccoon.

It was more than the bounty now. It was personal.

Wendy sat up and cast off his blankets. "Nature's call," he said sleepily, and with his elephant gun cradled in his arm, he shambled toward the woods.

Again Fargo yawned. His eyelids were leaden. He shook his head and slapped his cheek but it did no good. Annoyed, he got up and paced and flapped his arms to get his blood flowing.

The Ovaro raised its head and pricked its ears and nickered.

Fargo stopped flapping. The stallion was staring to the east. Wendy had gone north so it couldn't be the Brit. He looked but didn't see anything. Picking up his Sharps, he moved to the edge of the firelight. Nothing moved. There were no sounds.

The Ovaro was still staring—but to the south.

Fargo returned to the fire and added logs so the ring of light spread. He didn't spot any glowing eyes.

The Ovaro was looking to the west now.

Whatever was out there, Fargo realized, was circling. It could be anything. A wolf, a coyote, a fox, a deer.

The Ovaro lowered its head and went back to dozing.

Thank God, Fargo thought. They had been through enough for one day. He wondered what was keeping Wendy and thought about calling his name but that would wake the others. He sat down and checked the coffee. It was hot enough. Filling his tin cup, he leaned back and sipped. The warmth was welcome. So was the new vitality that flowed through his veins. But it didn't last. He swore in frustration.

"Somethin' the matter?" Cecelia was peering at him over her blanket.

"Tired, is all."

"I can keep watch if you want to lie down."

"Go back to sleep." Fargo placed the Sharps in his lap.

"I keep waking up," Cecelia said. "It's my side. It hurts somethin' awful."

"You're holding up better than most would." Fargo waggled his tin cup. "Care for some?"

"Don't mind if I do. Hold on." Cecelia grunted, propped her elbows under her, and slowly sat up. "Damn," she said, her face pinched. "That made me dizzy."

"Go slow for a while."

"I'll try, but I never have liked to lie around doin' nothin'." Cecelia paused. "I'm sorry about your friend. He was an ornery cuss but I liked him."

Fargo frowned.

"Guess I shouldn't have mentioned him. What else would you like to talk about? The weather?" Bethany stirred, and Cecelia tenderly pulled the girl's blanket higher. "I made a terrible mistake," she said so softly Fargo barely heard. "I shouldn't have come on this hunt."

"You can't blame yourself for what happened."

"I can blame myself for whatever I like." Cecelia touched her daughter's cheek. "Worse, it could have been my precious, here, or either of the boys. I wasn't thinkin' straight. I wanted the money. Wanted it more than anythin'. I put my kids' lives at risk for a few dollars."

"More than a few."

Cecelia's eyes misted over. "It could be a million and it wouldn't be enough if I lost them." She looked down at her side. "This could have been one of them instead of me. That griz almost had us. If I hadn't've flung that brand in its face . . ." She stopped.

"You did and all of you are alive."

"Damn it. Don't try to make me feel better. I did wrong and my kids came close to dyin' and I'll never forgive myself for bein' so stupid."

"We all do stupid things."

"Cut it out, I say." Cecelia straightened and winced. "I'm glad I hurt so much. Every twinge will remind me to put my children before everythin' else." She gave a slight shake and tilted her face to the heavens. "It sure is pretty in the high country, ain't it?"

Moose abruptly sat up and looked around in confusion. "I thought I heard your voice. What's going on? Why ain't you sleeping?"

"I couldn't so I've been bendin' Skye's ear," Cecelia quietly replied.

"Well, you can bend mine." Moose blinked his eyes and rubbed his beard. "I should go dip my head in the stream to wake up."

"No need. I'm goin' to lie back down here," Cecelia said. "I get tired too easy."

"It's about my turn to stand watch anyway," Moose said, and cast off his blanket.

"I'll be glad when we're back in town and don't have to worry about bein' attacked."

"You don't have to worry now," Moose said. "I'm here to protect you."

"That's sweet of . . ." Cecelia stopped and her eyes widened. "God, no."

Fargo heard a grunt, and turned.

It was Brain Eater.

21

The giant grizzly didn't roar or growl or rear; it exploded toward them.

Fargo barely had time to leap to his feet. The Sharps was next to him and he grabbed it as he rose and jammed it to his shoulder. He started to curl the hammer back as his vision filled with hair and teeth.

Cecelia shouted his name.

A blow to his chest sent Fargo flying. He lost his hold on the rifle as he tumbled end over end and came to rest with the world fading from black to firelight and to black again. Dimly, he heard the screams of the children, heard Moose bellow and the boom of a rifle, and a war whoop. He got his hands under him and made it to his knees.

The bear had Moose by the leg and was shaking him as a cat might a mouse. The big bear hunter, his features twisted in agony, was belaboring the grizzly's head and neck with his rifle.

Bird Rattler was striking with his tomahawk. Lazy Husband had notched an arrow.

Cecelia was too weak to do more than clutch Bethany and Thomas to her. "Shoot it!" she yelled, but not at Moose.

Abner had picked up her rifle and was cocking it. He thumbed the hammer back and raised the barrel so the muzzle was pointed at Brain Eater's head.

No, Fargo wanted to shout, go for the body. But as he opened his mouth the rifle went off.

Brain Eater let go of Moose and a forepaw flashed. The ruptured and crumpled body that landed ten feet from the fire bore little resemblance to the boy who had enraged it.

Cecelia and Bethany screamed.

Fargo heaved erect. He drew his Colt but didn't have a shot.

Bird Rattler was in his way. The tomahawk had bit deep again and again with no more effect than a pinprick. But now the bear took notice, and the sweep of a paw pinwheeled the Blackfoot to the earth. Brain Eater turned to finish him off but suddenly Moose was on his good leg and pointing a pistol.

"Die, damn you!"

The pistol spewed lead and smoke and the slug took the bear in the neck.

Brain Eater reared. As big as Moose was, the bear towered over him. Moose drew his long knife and plunged the blade into her body, hollering, "You won't hurt them, you hear me! Over my dead body!" He drew out the knife and stabbed again.

By then Fargo had a clear shot at the grizzly's throat. He fired twice and saw blood spurt.

Bird Rattler was back in the fray, hacking at the bear's head and body.

Moose dodged a raking paw and stabbed with fierce vigor, burying his knife to the hilt.

Fargo saw Cecelia attempting to scramble back and he ran to her and looped his hands under her arms. "I've got you," he said, and dragged her away, Bethany and Thomas clinging tight.

"Moose!" Cecelia screamed.

Fargo looked up.

Brain Eater had a huge paw on either side of Moose's head.

Moose was struggling mightily but the grizzly was too strong.

"Like hell!" he raged. "Like hell, like hell, like hell!"

And with each "hell" he drove his knife into her.

Brain Eater opened her maw. Fargo thought she was going to bite Moose on the head but she went for his neck. Moose stabbed and punched and tried to twist from her grip and then her fangs were at his jugular. Scarlet gushed, and Moose uttered a gurgling cry and went limp.

"Nooooooo!" Cecelia wailed.

Fargo let go of her. He had spotted his Sharps. He ran to it and scooped the rifle up.

Moose was down, his body convulsing. Brain Eater swatted at his head.

From behind the bear, Bird Rattler rushed. He had a lance. He drove it into her for fully half its length and wrenched it out so he could drive it into her again. But with a hideous roar Brain

Eater wheeled. Her paw caught the warrior across the face, her claws shearing through Bird Rattler's eyes and nose and lips.

Fargo fired. He aimed at the heart. Only a heart shot would drop her quick. But he must have missed because she spun and saw him and charged. Skipping backward, he dropped the Sharps and resorted once again to his Colt. He fired, nearly tripped, and fired once more. She was almost on top of him. He threw himself to one side just as a paw slammed into his leg. Upended, he described a high arc that ended with the thud of his body on the ground. A black pit sucked at him and he fought to stay conscious.

Bethany was screaming.

Thomas bawled, "Ma! Ma! Ma!"

A gun cracked.

Fargo pushed but had no strength. The black pit consumed him, and there was only silence.

Something was crawling on his face.

Fargo opened his eyes and wished he hadn't. Sunlight seared them like burning flame. They watered and his vision blurred and he shut them. The prickle of tiny legs left his cheek and a fly buzzed his ear. He was aware of the smell of the earth under his cheek, and another smell. His head hurt.

His chest and leg hurt worse. He couldn't get his mind to work as it should, and in his befuddled state he was unsure where he was or what had happened.

A whimper reminded him.

Fargo tensed to rise, and caught himself. The bear might be nearby. He cracked his lids and saw what was left of Bird Rattler a few yards away. The warrior's head had been split like a melon and his brain was gone.

The whimper was repeated.

Fargo slowly turned his head. Cecelia was on her back, her arm bent at an unnatural angle, her fingers hooked as if she were scratching at the air. Blood framed her in a pool.

Fargo gambled. He raised his head. Brain Eater was nowhere to be seen. Bodies were, though. Bird Rattler. Lazy Husband—his brain had been eaten, too. Moose. Abner, with half a head. A smaller pile of mangled flesh and shattered bones must be Thomas.

A legion of flies swarmed them.

Fargo pushed to his knees. He had been out for hours. The

sun was straight overhead. The front of his shirt was torn and he had claw marks on his chest. His left leg had deeper cuts and was slightly numb. When he stood the leg nearly gave out. He shuffled over to Cecelia and nearly stepped on her intestines.

The grizzly had ripped her open from sternum to hip. That she had lasted as long as she had was a tribute to her will.

Fargo eased down, gently clasped her hand, and said her name.

Cecelia's eyes opened. They were mirrors to horror beyond reckoning. She tried twice to say something and managed, "Skye?"

"I'm sorry."

"For what? It wasn't your fault." Cecelia swallowed and winced.

"Why am I still alive?"

"Why are . . . either of us?" Cecelia weakly rejoined. "The bear . . . ate their brains . . . and then left."

Fargo needed a gun. The grizzly might come back. He started to turn but she gripped his hand so tight, it hurt.

"Wait. You have . . . to save her."

"Who?" Fargo said, and knew the moment he asked.

"Beth. She got away . . . I think. I told her to run. She went that way . . ." Cecelia tried to point toward the stream. "You must find her."

"I will," Fargo vowed.

"I don't have any kin who would take her," Cecelia gasped. "Get her to an orphanage. Or a minister or a priest."

"I'll see she's taken care of."

Cecelia smiled and closed her eyes. "Thank you. I'm afraid I don't have long left."

"Don't worry. I'll stay with you."

"No," Cecelia said. "Forget about me. Find Bethany. She must be scared to . . ." She stopped and inhaled.

"For what it's worth, you're a fine mother," Fargo sought to ease her regret. "You did what you thought best." He squeezed her hand but she didn't squeeze back. "Cecelia?" He pressed his fingers to her wrist; she had no pulse. "Damn." He slowly stood and surveyed the slaughter. He saw his Sharps. As he was reloading it he remembered the horses.

They were gone.

Fargo went over to where they had been tied. There was no

blood, which told him they ran off and weren't killed. He'd trained the Ovaro to come when he whistled and he whistled several times but the stallion didn't appear. He moved to the stream and hollered for Bethany over and over, with the same result.

Kneeling, Fargo undid his bandanna. He soaked it and washed each of his cuts to reduce the risk of them festering. He washed his face, wrung the bandanna out, and retied it. Standing, he shouted for Bethany and whistled for the Ovaro, and shouted louder. He was about to turn when the undergrowth to his left crackled. Snapping the Sharps to his shoulder, he aimed at moving brush.

Out of the thicket shuffled Wendolyn. His shirt and pants were ripped and stained with blood and he had cuts on his upper arm that could use stitches. He was holding his elephant gun limply at his side. He mustered a lopsided grin and said, "Miss me?" His legs started to buckle.

Fargo caught him and lowered him onto his back. "I figured the bear got you, too."

"I never heard it," Wendy said. "I had just got done buttoning up and it was on me." He stopped. "Wait. Did you say 'too'? How many of the others?"

"All of them except you and me and maybe the little girl," Fargo informed him.

Shock made the Brit paler than he already was. "No," he said. "Not that remarkable woman and her adorable boys."

"Here," Fargo said, undoing his bandanna again. "Let me clean you up."

The blow to Wendy's head had cut half an inch deep. Fargo cleaned the slashes and the other wounds and cut a strip from Wendy's shirt to use as a bandage. The Brit lay quiet until he was done.

"I'm sorry. I shouldn't have let myself be taken so easily."

"A grizzly is a ghost when it wants to be."

"I should have been at your side. Together we could have saved them."

"Or you could be lying over there with your brains eaten out."

"I never expected . . ." Wendy paused. "I thought bears were blundering, noisy beasts. Of all the animals I've hunted, this grizzly of yours reminds me most of a tiger. Its stealth belies its bulk and its cunning is second to none."

"That pretty much describes a grizzly, all right," Fargo said.

"I've underestimated my enemy and now those poor people have paid for my mistake."

"Quit beating yourself over it."

Grimacing, Wendy sat up. "This beast has to be stopped. We have to kill this blighter."

"Dead as dead can be," Fargo agreed.

22

They spent the better part of an hour searching for Bethany, yelling her name until they were hoarse. Then they attended to the bodies. The best they could do was cover them. All except Cecelia. Wendolyn insisted on burying her even though they had nothing to dig with except branches and rocks. They scooped a shallow grave and Wendy bowed his head.

"In the sweat of your face you shall eat bread until you return to the ground. For out of it were you taken. For dust you are, and to dust you shall return."

Fargo waited, and when the Brit didn't go on, he said, "Was that the Bible?"

Wendy nodded and shouldered his elephant gun.

"Is that all you're going to say?"

"What else is there?"

The patches of blood still crawled with flies. Fargo kindled a new fire near where the lean-to had been. The coffeepot was intact and half full, and he put it on to heat.

The Britisher squatted across from him. "Let's assess our situation. Everyone else is dead. Our horses have run off. Most of our supplies have been destroyed. We're both wounded and hurting. Brain Eater is still out there somewhere and could show up at any moment. Is there anything I missed?"

"There's a storm coming," Fargo said, and pointed to the west where a thunderhead framed the horizon. Flashes of lightning danced in the dark clouds.

"Just what we need," Wendy said. "A good drenching."

"It'll be a couple of hours yet," Fargo said. "We'll finish the coffee and hunt cover to wait it out."

"What then? Do we go after the bear on foot?"

"I don't think we'll have to," Fargo replied. "When she's ready she'll come for us."

"Tigers do the same thing," Wendy said. "They turn on you, and the hunter becomes the hunted." He closed his eyes and touched the bandage on his head.

"You all right?"

"I keep having dizzy spells. They don't last long but they're a nuisance."

Fargo had problems of his own. His hip was stiff and his leg so sore he could barely stand to put his full weight on it. "We're not in much shape for bear-killing."

"We have to outthink the monster. You know these animals better than I do. Come up with an idea that will give us an edge."

"That's a tall order," Fargo said. But he put his mind to it as they sat sipping coffee and listening to the distant rumble of thunder.

The wind picked up, bringing with it the scent of moisture. The sky darkened and the thunder grew louder.

They collected all the weapons and saddles and what was left of their supplies and put everything under a spruce. Its thick limbs would ward off most of the rain. For their own shelter Fargo chose a hollow overhang by the bank of the stream. As the first drops fell, they hunkered with their backs to bare earth.

Lightning speared the sky and thunder shook the ground. The firmament opened and unleashed a torrent, the rain so heavy they couldn't see more than a few feet.

Fargo felt an occasional cool drop on his face and the lash of the wind but otherwise he was snug as a bedbug in a quilt.

The stream flowed faster, its surface pockmarked. A piece of wood went floating past, and shortly after, a frog.

Wendy had his arm across his chest and his elephant gun across his lap. He began trembling and rubbed his hands together.

"You cold?"

"Like a block of ice," the Brit confirmed.

Fargo frowned. The temperature hadn't fallen more than a couple of degrees. He wondered if infection was setting in. It was common with animal bites, and often fatal.

"When we are back to Gold Creek, the first thing I am going to do is take a hot bath," Wendy said. "I may stay in the tub for a month."

"You'll be the talk of the town," Fargo joked. "Most men don't take but one bath a year and keep it as short as they can."

"I've noticed that about you Yanks. Moose, God rest his soul, had an atrocious stink. And those Blackfeet had a peculiar smell about them, as well."

"That was the bear fat."

"I beg your pardon?" Wendy said.

"Some tribes rub bear grease in their hair to make it shine. One uses red clay. In the Southwest there's a tribe that's fond of smearing their hair with pulp they dig out of a cactus. Another uses buffalo shit sometimes."

"My word. That's barbaric."

"By your standards," Fargo said.

"Here now," Wendy said. "By any standard, to use buffalo excrement in one's hair is despicable."

"Some use piss."

"I'm beginning to suspect that you're making this up. No one in their right mind would do that."

Fargo was about to say that people made do with what was on hand when he sensed movement in the rain. He looked, and a tingle ran down his spine.

Something was coming toward them.

Fargo stayed still. Whatever it was, odds were it hadn't seen them. Wendy went to speak and Fargo put his finger to his lips and then pointed at the vague shape in the rain. All they could tell was that it was big.

The thing stopped in front of the hollow.

Fargo placed both hands on his Sharps. Whatever it was, it knew they were there.

Wendy motioned at his elephant gun and at the creature and pantomimed shooting it.

Fargo shook his head.

Wendy silently mouthed the words, "Why not?"

As if to answer him, the rain parted and the Ovaro stuck its head under the overhang.

"I'll be damned," Wendy said.

Fargo's joy was boundless. Reaching up, he patted the stallion's neck. "It's good to see you again." The stallion nuzzled him and he scratched around its ears and under its jaw.

There was more movement, and a second and third horse clustered at the opening.

"Our lucky day," Wendy beamed, patting one.

Thunderstorms in the high country swept in swiftly and just as swiftly swept off to the east. Already the rain was slackening and the lightning flashed less.

Fargo stayed put until the drizzle dwindled to random drops. Emerging, he led the Ovaro and another horse over to the spruce. Wendolyn brought the third. When Fargo bent and picked up his saddle blanket, he said, "Going somewhere?"

"Bethany," was all Fargo had to say.

Two hours of daylight remained, enough for them to sweep in a wide circle. The rain washed away any tracks the girl made but Fargo had to try. Twilight was falling when he reined toward the meadow.

"I kept hoping Brain Eater will have another go at us," Wendy said.

"Be careful what you hope for."

Gathering enough dry wood to last the night took a long time. For supper they had coffee and beans. Fargo was ravenous and had two helpings. He was spooning up the last of the sauce when Wendy cleared his throat.

"What are your plans for tomorrow?"

"We'll look for the girl again. Yell our fool heads off and hope to hell she hears us."

Wendy looked uncomfortable saying, "And if we don't find her? How long do we keep at it? The day after, as well? A week? When do we say enough is enough and get to the business of destroying Brain Eater?"

"We owe it to Cecelia," Fargo said.

"I know that. I'm only saying that as much as we would like to find the child, we must face the possibility that we won't. The bear might have got her."

"So long as there's hope we keep at it."

They took turns sitting guard. Wendy insisted on the first watch, saying he wasn't tired.

Fargo lay on his side and tried to drift off but his mind was racing from all that had happened. He relived Bear Eater's attack in his mind's eye and couldn't think of anything he could have done differently to save those who died.

Death came in many shapes and guises in the wild. It came without warning, without mercy. One moment a man was minding his own business and the next he was fighting for his life.

Fargo would have thought that by now he would be used to it, but he wasn't.

An owl was hooting when sleep claimed him. It seemed not five minutes had gone by when a hand was on his shoulder, shaking him, and a voice was urgently whispering for him to wake up. He opened his eyes. "What is it?"

"We have company," Wendy said.

Fargo sat up. He heard it right away: crashing off in the woods to the west. It sounded like a herd of buffalo were plowing through the vegetation but there were no buffs that high up. He laid a hand on his Sharps.

"What can it be?" Wendy asked. "I haven't heard any gnarls or roars."

As if to prove him wrong, an ominous growl was carried on the wind.

"Brain Eater," Fargo said, and stood.

"You're sure?" Wendy pushed up. "Why is she making all that noise?"

"You'd have to ask her."

"I'm serious."

"So am I." Fargo had no idea what the grizzly was up to.

He'd never heard of a bear throwing a tantrum but that sounded like what she was doing. Or maybe, he mused, she was working herself up to attack them. Or—and the thought chilled him—she was deliberately making all that noise to draw them away from the fire.

The sounds went on for a while. Tree limbs snapping, brush crackling and popping. Now and again the bear growled. Finally the sounds subsided and the forest was quiet.

"I say, did she leave?" Wendy wondered.

Minutes dragged by and the silence continued.

Fargo sat back down and reached for his tin cup. He couldn't go back to sleep knowing the man-killer might be watching and waiting for her chance to strike.

"I don't mind admitting these grizzlies of yours wreak havoc with my nerves," Wendy said as he reached for his own cup.

"They'll do that."

"Tigers, rhinos, lions, you name it, all behave in certain ways. Even rogue elephants are predictable. You know what to expect." Wendy stared into the darkness. "But not these great bloody bears. No animal I've ever hunted on any continent acts like they do."

Fargo was watching the Ovaro. It would alert him if the griz came close.

"I never know what Brain Eater will do next," Wendolyn said. "She seems to delight in bedeviling us."

"No seems about it," Fargo said.

"It's damned near demonic."

"There's only one thing you can be sure of with a grizzly," Fargo said.

"What might that be?"

"That it will kill you dead."

23

Fargo was curious. As soon as they were up and ate and saddled, he rode west into the trees. Fifty feet in he came on flattened brush and broken branches and trees with claw and teeth marks. Brain Eater's tracks were everywhere.

"It's as if she went berserk," Wendy said.

Fargo dismounted and led the Ovaro by the reins. The griz had torn a five- to six-foot swatch at the base of a knoll. He followed the path of destruction and discovered it went completely around the knoll so that soon he was back where he started. The knoll was bare except for a jumble of boulders at the top. "Cover me."

The two largest boulders were giant slabs that leaned against one another. Between them was a gap half as wide as Fargo's shoulders. Hunkering, he peered in. He couldn't see anything. He reached in and felt empty space. As he was drawing his hand out he thought he heard a sniffle. A tingle of excitement ran through him. "Bethany?"

The sniffle was repeated.

"Bethany?" Fargo said again.

"The girl is alive?" Wendy exclaimed, and was off his horse and up the knoll beside him.

Fargo motioned for quiet. Bending lower, he thought he detected movement. "It's Skye, Bethany. You know me."

The movement coalesced into a pale face streaked with tear tracks and dirt. "Skye?" she said timidly.

"We've been looking all over for you," Fargo said. "Didn't you hear us calling?"

Bethany nodded.

"Why didn't you answer us?"

"I was scared."

"Of the bear?"

Bethany nodded, and gulped.

"She's gone. It's just Mr. Wendolyn and me. It's safe for you to come out."

"Where's my ma?"

"Oh," Fargo said, jolted by the realization that she didn't know.

"Where is she? Why isn't she with you?"

"God," Wendy said.

"Bethany," Fargo said softly. "I'm afraid it's just the three of us—" He got no further.

The girl's face disappeared and racking sobs came out of the hole. "No, no, no, no, no."

Wendy sat on a small boulder and leaned on his elephant gun. "I've never wanted to kill anything as much as I do this bloody beast."

Fargo waited for Beth to cry herself out. It was a long wait. When all he heard were sniffles, he turned to the hole. "Bethany? You need to come out now."

She didn't respond.

"Please."

"Go away," Bethany said.

"Not without you. You can't stay here by yourself. You'll starve or the bear will get you."

"I don't care."

"Don't talk like that."

"Ma is gone. Abner's gone. Thomas is gone." Bethany mewed in despair. "I'm all alone."

"There is Wendy and me. We'll see to it that you get to town and we'll find someone to look after you."

"Who? There's no one left but me."

"Come on out."

"No."

Fargo sat back. He was trying to be patient with her but Brain Eater was out there somewhere. "Bethany, your ma wouldn't want you to do this. She didn't tell you to run so you could hide in a hole and die. She wanted you to live."

"What's the use?" the girl said plaintively.

"You die and there will be no one to remember your ma. How good she was. How much she cared for you. There will be no one to remember Abner and Thomas. Is that what you want?"

"I loved my ma."

"And she loved you."

"I loved my brothers too."

Her face reappeared, her cheeks and chin wet from her crying. "You won't let the bear kill me, will you? It tried and tried but couldn't reach me."

Fargo glanced at the crushed vegetation below. That explained the grizzly's tantrum. "We'll do all we can to protect you." He spread his arms and smiled. "Please come out."

Suddenly she was pressed to his chest and sobbing anew. She clung to him with her face in his shirt, her small frame racked by violent shaking.

Wendy coughed and looked away.

Fargo held her until she became quiet and still. "Beth?" he said softly.

She didn't reply.

Fargo leaned down. Exhaustion and hunger and sorrow had taken their toll; she was sound asleep.

"I'll be," Wendy said.

"This changes everything."

Wendy nodded. "We can't very well go off after the bear with her to look after. We'll have to take her to town and come back." He sighed. "It could be weeks before we find the bear again."

"It can't be helped," Fargo said.

"Any idea who you can leave her with?"

"There's a church. Maybe the parson will know of someone." Fargo carried her down the knoll. He had Wendy hold her while he mounted, then the Brit handed her up. She was so small that he could hold her in one arm.

"Look at her," Wendy said, smiling. "The little angel."

Fargo reined around.

"You know," Wendy said as they rode. "Since we're going back anyway, we might as well spend a few days resting up. I can have that bath. Is there anything you'd like to do?"

Fargo thought of Fanny. "Yes."

"We'll buy more supplies and return to the fray refreshed. What do you say?"

By then they had reached the meadow. Wisps of smoke rose from the embers of their fire. The third horse was where they had left it, grazing.

Behind the horse, just coming out of the trees, was Brain Eater.

The very instant that Fargo set eyes on the giant grizzly, she roared and charged. The sorrel burst into flight. For a split second only the picket pin slowed her. But that moment proved costly. The pin came out and the sorrel was in flight but the bear was on her. Iron jaws ripped her flank. A front paw caught her rear leg. The sorrel stumbled and the bear was on her. The horse squealed at the impact. Meat-eater and prey crashed to the ground. Frantic, the sorrel tried to rise but the bear's maw closed on her throat.

Fargo's Sharps was in his saddle scabbard and he couldn't grab it with Bethany in his arm.

Wendy, though, snapped the elephant gun to his shoulder. He took careful aim, saying, "I've got you now, you ungodly brute."

Brain Eater hadn't noticed them yet. She was tearing and ripping at the sorrel. Blood spurted like rain, soaking the bear's head and hump.

Tiny fingers clutched at Fargo's buckskin shirt. Bethany was awake and frozen in terror.

Fargo wondered what Wendy was waiting for; he probably wanted to be sure of a kill shot. But if he took too long and the grizzly spotted them—

Brain Eater looked right at them and let out a loud *woof* of surprise. A chunk of horseflesh and hide hung from her mouth. Dropping it, she started over the horse toward them.

Wendy fired. The two-bore boomed and bucked, and so did his mount. He grabbed at the saddle to keep from being thrown and almost dropped the elephant gun.

Fargo's gaze was glued to the bear. She had stopped as if she'd slammed into a wall. He thought the slug hit her in the chest but he couldn't be sure. She looked down at herself and then at them. Roaring, she charged.

"Hell," Fargo said, and reined around. "Light a shuck!" he shouted, and galloped into the woods. Bethany flung her arms around his neck and bleated like a stricken lamb. Fargo glanced back.

Wendolyn was trying to turn his horse but it was giving him trouble. It saw the grizzly rushing toward them and wheeled on its own. Instead of following the Ovaro, though, it bolted in a different direction.

The grizzly stopped and looked after each horse and chose to pursue Wendy's.

Fargo reined after them. The Brit was a good rider but it would take considerable skill to stay ahead of Brain Eater, as he had learned the hard way. He heard the bear roar and the crash of undergrowth. Wendy was shouting but Fargo couldn't make out the words.

Bethany began crying into Fargo's neck and whimpering.

Fargo couldn't take the time to comfort her. He concentrated on riding and only on riding. He glimpsed a gigantic brown form and would have lashed the reins for the Ovaro to go faster were it not that he had to hold on to Bethany or she would fall.

Wendy had stopped yelling. Fargo lost sight of the bear. He continued in the direction they had been going and was startled a minute later when a roar split the wilds from off to the east. He reined down the mountain and after several minutes drew rein to listen and look.

Bethany had stopped crying and was gazing fearfully about with tear-filled eyes. "Where are they?" she whispered.

Fargo didn't know. It was quiet—too quiet. "They have to be near here." Scouring the terrain, he rode on. He was tempted to call Wendy's name but the grizzly might hear and come after them.

Bethany pressed her cheek to his. "I'm scared."

"So am I."

"You are? But you're a man and you have guns."

"I bleed like anybody else," Fargo said.

"Ma liked you," the girls said out of the blue.

"I liked her, too."

"She said if she didn't have Moose she wouldn't mind being your woman."

"Did she, now?" Fargo was listening intently.

"Would you have liked Ma to be?"

Fargo looked at her. "Any man would." He was rewarded with a smile.

The faint crack of what might be a limb put an end to their

talk. Fargo descended another quarter of a mile but saw only birds and a squirrel. He began a broader search. They entered a stand of mixed pines, the trees so closely spaced that he couldn't see more than a dozen yards. A groan caused him to draw rein.

"Did you hear that?" the girl whispered.

"Shhhh." Fargo positioned her so she was on his left hip and he could get at his holster quickly if need be.

Another groan rose.

Fargo went past more trees. Suddenly the Ovaro shied. There, in the grass, lay the Brit, his hat gone and a deep gash on his forehead. His elephant gun was a few feet away. Fargo didn't see his horse—or the bear.

Sliding off, Fargo lowered Bethany. "Stay close," he cautioned. He needn't have bothered. She glued herself to his leg.

"Wendy?" Fargo said, kneeling. He lightly slapped the hunter's cheek. "Can you hear me?"

Wendolyn's eyes opened and he winced and said, "Bloody hell."

"What happened? Where's Brain Eater?"

"Gone, I hope." Wendy rose onto his elbows and gingerly placed a hand on the new wound. "The brute chased off after my horse."

"You jumped off to save yourself?"

Wendy started to shake his head and winced. "I wish I could claim to be that clever. But no, I was knocked off by a tree limb."

"It may have saved your life," Fargo said. "You don't look too bad off." The gash wasn't bleeding and there wasn't any other wound that he could find.

"It didn't do my head any favors." Wendy sat up, with help, and hung his head in misery. "I feel sick. It wouldn't surprise me if I had a concussion."

"You'll be all right, mister," Bethany said. "We'll fix you."

Wendy looked at her and smiled. "I'd almost forgotten about you, child. Now there are the three of us but only one horse."

"We'll look for yours," Fargo said. He picked up the elephant gun and had Wendy climb on the Ovaro. Then he handed up the rifle and went to lift Bethany.

"No," she said. "I want to be with you."

"I need my hands free."

"I like you," she said.

"It's for your own good."

"Please."

Fargo looked at the Brit, who shrugged.

"I remember Fanny saying that you have a way with the ladies."

"Who's Fanny?" Bethany asked.

"A friend." Fargo held her on his left hip and the reins in his right hand and followed a trail of crushed grass and brush. It went for almost a mile, to the crest of a ridge. There, the tracks diverged. The hoofprints went on down the mountain toward the creek while the bear's tracks bore to the south into heavy forest. "Your horse got away."

"Good for him."

Bears were fast over short distances but lacked stamina. Fargo imagined that Brain Eater was holed up somewhere, resting and licking her wounds. That reminded him. "I know you hit her when you shot."

"Yet she didn't go down." Wendy ruefully regarded his elephant gun. "I've dropped bull elephants and cape buffalo with one shot but not this bloody bear."

"Grizzlies are tough," Fargo said.

"If you ask me, this one is damn near indestructible." Wendy gazed at the timber. "Do you think she's had enough or will she come after us?"

Fargo looked at Bethany. "I wouldn't relax just yet," he said.

24

That evening they camped at the base of a cliff. To one side was a pile of boulders twenty feet high. To the other was the game trail they had followed down. That was likely how Brain Eater would approach, so Fargo sat facing the trail with the Sharps close to his right leg and the elephant gun close to his left.

Wendy was in no condition to shoot. The Brit had been nauseous and dizzy most of the day and now lay with his head propped on a rolled-up blanket, gazing glumly into the fire.

Bethany was curled up asleep under another blanket, only her hair showing.

Fargo added several pieces of wood to the fire. For supper they'd had pemmican and a few swallows of water. His canteen was only a third full so he hadn't made coffee. "You should try to get some sleep."

"I hate this," Wendy said. "I feel next to helpless. It shouldn't all be on your shoulders."

"By tomorrow you might feel better," Fargo tried to encourage him.

"I hope so." Wendy hesitated. "I haven't said anything but I've been blacking out for short spells, half a minute or so. My mind shuts down and then I'm conscious again. I don't know what to make of it."

Fargo hid his concern. The Brit needed a doctor and the only sawbones in five hundred miles was in Gold Creek. Even if they pushed hard it would take two days to get there. "Just take it easy."

"I can help keep watch at least."

"No," Fargo said. All they needed was for Wendy to black out when Brain Eater was stalking them.

"I tell you, I—" Wendy's chin dipped to his chest. His chest rose and fell rhythmically in the measured breathing of deep sleep.

Fargo swore. They were in a bad way. Little water, not much food, one of them hurt severely and the other a small girl, only one horse between them and a killer bear somewhere near. "Can it get any worse?" he asked the air. He knew the answer.

The night crawled. Several times Fargo got up and paced.

Along about four in the morning he was overcome with drowsiness and his head lolled. He told himself that he must get up and move around, but the next he knew, he opened his eyes and squinted in the bright glare of the morning sun. It had been up a couple of hours.

Wendy and Bethany were still asleep.

Fargo stretched and stood. Birds were singing. Far below the blue of the creek stood out against the green of the woodland. Reluctantly, he woke the Brit. He had to shake him a while before Wendy's eyes fluttered open.

"Is that you, Yank? I was having the most wonderful dream."

"How do you feel?"

"Too soon to tell."

Bethany jerked at Fargo's touch, then sat up. She scratched her hair and looked around and said, "Oh."

Fargo passed out more pemmican for breakfast. When they were done he boosted Wendy onto the Ovaro and swung Bethany up.

He slid the Sharps into the scabbard and held on to the elephant gun.

The slope below was treacherous. Fargo picked their way with care. The stallion, as sure-footed as it was, experienced a few slips and slides. He was glad when they reached the bottom.

Fargo gazed over his shoulder—and his blood became ice.

A giant form was silhouetted on top of the cliff. It was in shadow and the head and neck were indistinguishable from the dark block of body but there was no confusing it for an elk or some other animal.

Brain Eater wheeled and plunged into the forest.

It happened so fast, Fargo half wondered if he'd imagined it. But no, she was shadowing them. He continued on down. That she hadn't attacked was encouraging. She might hold off until dark.

Wendy kept passing out. The next time he did his arm slipped from around Bethany and she would have fallen had Fargo not caught her. He set her down and walked with her hand in his.

In a while Wendolyn straightened and frowned. "Sorry."

"When you need to stop and rest, say so."

Fargo checked behind them so many times, he got a crick in his neck. Brain Eater didn't show.

Miles to the south, gray smudges against the blue sky marked where tendrils of smoke rose from town.

Fargo wondered if he would ever see it again.

Another night washed dark and chill over the vastness of the northern Rockies. The carnivores emerged and the timberland echoed with their roars and cries.

Fargo camped beside a spring in a sheltered nook.

Uncomfortably close brambles hemmed it on three sides. He didn't like the spot but they had been without water all day.

Now he had coffee on to brew. Wendy was on a blanket with an arm over his eyes. Bethany swirled a stick in the spring.

"I feel bloody awful," Wendy lamented.

"By midnight tomorrow we'll reach Gold Creek."

Wendy placed his arm on his chest. He was drawn and haggard and ungodly pale. He'd refused a bite to eat, saying he was too queasy to keep it down.

Bethany stood and threw the stick into the darkness. Coming around the fire, she surprised Fargo by plopping into his lap. "Tell me a story."

"A what?"

"Ma always told us a story before we went to bed. I'd like to go to sleep so tell me one."

Fargo was taken aback. Most of the "stories" he knew would get belly laughs in a saloon but weren't fit for children.

"You must know one," Bethany said. "A fairy tale would be nice. Ma liked fairy tales."

Fargo racked his brain. He recollected his mother had told a few when he was young but he would be damned if he could remember them. "How about the goat and the turtle?"

Bethany smiled and squirmed excitedly. "I never heard that one. How does it go?"

"Once upon a time"—Fargo remembered most fairy tales began that way—"there was a goat and a turtle. One day the goat was walking along and he saw a turtle and said 'howdy.'"

"Howdy?" Wendy said with his eyes closed, and snorted.

"That's how goats talk," Fargo told Beth. "Just then it started to rain. The goat was wet and cold but the turtle pulled into his shell until the rain stopped and then poked his head out again."

"I saw a turtle do that," Bethany said.

"The goat liked the shell. It kept the turtle dry. He wanted a shell for himself so he went out back of a house where an old woman had hung her laundry and pulled a blanket down with his teeth and swung it over his back."

"Gosh," Bethany said.

"He went to the turtle to show him. He bragged how his shell was bigger and better than the turtle's. Just then it rained again. The blanket was soaked. So was the goat. The turtle laughed so hard, the goat got mad and stomped on him and the turtle died."

"Oh, the poor turtle."

"The moral of the story is don't poke fun at people unless you want to be stomped."

"That was a good one," Beth said.

Wendolyn opened his eyes. "It was the sorriest excuse for a fairy tale I've ever heard."

"If you can do better be my guest."

"I have a joke I heard about three sailors and a farmer's daughter."

"Tell us," Bethany coaxed.

"Not on your life, little one."

Bethany pecked Fargo on the cheek. "Will you tuck me in like Ma used to do?"

Fargo tried to remember the last time, if ever, he'd tucked a child in. He pulled the blanket to her chin and patted her cheek. "If you need anything give a holler." He returned to his seat at the fire.

"The goat and the turtle?" Wendy said again, and indulged in quiet laughter.

"Go to hell," Fargo said.

Wendy's mirth died in his throat and he thrust a finger at the woods.

Eyeshine blazed where the brambles merged into the trees.

Fargo jumped up and jammed the elephant gun to his shoulder. It was the heaviest rifle he'd ever held. The Brit had to be a lot stronger than he looked to tote the thing around all day. Fargo sighted down the barrel—and the eyes disappeared.

"Was it Brain Eater, do you reckon?"

Fargo felt foolish. "I can't say," he admitted. But now that he thought about it, the eyes weren't as high off the ground as the grizzly's, nor as far apart.

"And me lying here useless," Wendy said.

Fargo edged toward the trees. A black bear wouldn't worry him. They scared easier than grizzlies. He came to where he thought it had been standing.

"Anything?" Wendy whispered.

"No."

The relief Fargo felt was short-lived. He came back into the circle of firelight just as a roar rolled down from the crags above.

25

"Now *that* was the bloody bear," Wendy exclaimed.

Fargo agreed. From the sound, Brain Eater was about a quarter of a mile off. Was she making a kill? Or letting them know she was still after them?

Bethany had sat up and was staring fearfully up the mountain. "Will she kill us like she did my ma?"

"I won't let her," Fargo said. "Lie back down and try to get some sleep."

She did as he told her, the blanket up to her nose, her eyes as wide as double eagles.

Fargo went over to the Brit. "How are you feeling?"

"Better and better. By morning I'll be in the prime of health."

Fargo placed his hand on Wendolyn's forehead. "You're burning up."

"A slight fever, nothing more. I insist on pulling my weight. I'll take second watch tonight."

"Like hell you will."

"You're making too much of a fuss. I'm perfectly capable, I tell you."

"The answer is still no." Fargo sat where he could see the woods and most of the brambles and placed the elephant gun across his lap. It was going to be a long night. He filled his cup with coffee and wet his throat.

"You're terribly stubborn, Yank." Wendy wouldn't let it drop. "Why can't you take my word for it?"

"Because you're a terrible liar."

"What if I stay up anyway?" Wendy challenged. "What if I help you stand watch all night?"

"You're welcome to try."

"All right, then," Wendy said angrily. "Just sit there and see if I don't."

In less than ten minutes both were sound asleep, Bethany's face cherubic in the starlight, Wendolyn snoring and sputtering and tossing.

The coffee helped but Fargo was worried he might not stay awake the whole night. An occasional crackle brought him to his feet but whatever was out there stayed out there. Deer, mostly, he reckoned. Once he saw eyes but it was a raccoon. "Shoo," he said, and stomped his foot, and the little bandit ran off.

By midnight Fargo had downed six cups. It was a wonder he didn't slosh when he moved. But the six weren't enough. His chin kept dipping to his chest and his eyes would close. He always snapped them open but each time it took longer than the last.

Midnight came and went. Fargo jerked his head up and swore. This time he had been out for several minutes. Brain Eater could have walked up to him and separated his head from his body and he'd never have known it. He picked up the coffeepot and shook it. Another three or four cups, he calculated, enough to last until morning. He poured and set the pot down and when he looked up, something was looking at him.

The creature was in the trees, far enough away that he couldn't tell what it was. The eyes were big enough and high enough— but was it Brain Eater? He set the cup down and reached for the elephant gun.

The eyes were coming closer.

Fargo cocked the hammer and remembered to firm his grip. The animal stopped just beyond the firelight. He wanted it to growl or roar so there wouldn't be any doubt. All it did was stand there. To hell with it, he thought, and took aim.

The animal took a few more steps.

"Damn," Fargo said. "I should shoot you anyway."

The cow elk seemed curious. She stared at him and the sleepers and at the Ovaro and then turned and walked off.

Fatigue set in again, and it was all Fargo could do to stay awake. He stood and walked around the fire. He slapped himself and pinched himself.

Wendy was sawing logs. Bethany had pulled the blanket up over her head.

A chill wind started to blow in from the north. Fargo was grateful. It revitalized him a little. Enough that he was still awake when a golden arc framed the eastern horizon.

He had done it. He had lasted the night. He let the Brit and the girl sleep in.

With the spreading light of the new day, his spirits rose. That Brain Eater hadn't attacked suggested the grizzly had made another kill. He hoped so, for their sake. It would keep the bear away a while.

They reached the creek about eleven.

Wendolyn knelt and splashed water on his head and neck. He claimed he was feeling better. As for Bethany, she sat staring sadly into space. Every now and again she would sniffle and say, "Ma."

While the Ovaro drank, Fargo prowled the bank and scanned the woods. He couldn't shake a persistent feeling the bear was close. He tried to tell himself it was nerves.

Wendy had wet a handkerchief and applied it to the gash on his head.

"Any dizziness this morning?" Fargo asked.

"Hardly any. All I needed was a good night's rest. Which reminds me. It was damned decent of you to let us sleep."

"You can return the favor tonight if we don't make it to Gold Creek."

A mile along they rounded a bend and came on a small shack, with a mule tied to a sapling. A sluice sat near the water.

As they passed the sluice the door opened and out strode an unkempt barrel of flab holding a shotgun.

"What the hell are you doing on my claim?"

"Passing through," Fargo said.

The man had the shotgun halfway to his shoulder when he blinked and said, "Wait. I know you. I saw you in town. You're that scout. The one who found the Nesmith family."

"That was me," Fargo confirmed.

"They were decent folks." The man lowered his shotgun. "Sorry for pointing this at you but a man has to protect his own."

Fargo was too tired to dally. "Be seeing you." He put another bend behind them, and suddenly stopped. "Damn it. I have to go back."

"What on earth for?" Wendy asked.

"To warn him," Fargo said. "If the grizzly is following us, he's in danger." He handed the elephant gun to Wendy so he could run faster. The shack door was open. Apparently the man had gone back in. "Mister?" he hollered. He got no answer. He went around the sluice and was almost to the shack when he saw red drops on the ground.

Stunned, Fargo stopped and placed his hand on his Colt. It couldn't be, he told himself. He hadn't heard a scream or a shout. He sidled to the left to see past the corner.

The shotgun lay in a scarlet pool. Drag marks led toward the trees.

Fargo heard a crunch. Shadows cloaked a huge shape that was tearing and biting. He backed away. When he was past the shack he whirled and flew along the creek. The Brit and the girl were still on the Ovaro, talking. He grabbed the elephant gun.

"What's wrong?" Wendy asked in alarm.

"Ride like hell."

Bewildered, Wendy gripped the strap to his ammo pouch, and paused. "It's Brain Eater, isn't it?"

"Don't stop until you reach town." Fargo was tired of running. "I'll hold her here as long as I can."

"What kind of bounder do you take me for?" Wendy said indignantly. "I'm staying to help."

"Think of her," Fargo said with a nod at Bethany.

"Why must it be you?"

"Go!" Fargo said.

Wendy angrily declared, "I am against this. I'm not a coward."

"Never said you were. Hold on to her."

"What?"

"Hold on to Beth," Fargo said, and gave the Ovaro a hard slap. The stallion broke into a trot. Wendy looked back and scowled as they disappeared around a stand of cottonwoods.

Fargo turned and sprinted back. He slowed when he neared the shack so the bear wouldn't hear. That was when he realized, to his shock, that he had forgotten to grab the Sharps. He drew the Colt. The crunching had stopped. He cautiously peered around the corner and almost swore out loud.

The grizzly was gone. Incredulous, Fargo crouched and glided toward the spot where he had last seen it. Any movement, however slight, caused him to freeze: the twitch of a leaf, the flutter of a butterfly, the flight of a sparrow. He smelled the blood before he saw the remains. An arm was severed, a leg mangled. The sternum had been opened like a breadbox, exposing the ribs and the organs underneath.

Fargo was astounded by how much damage the grizzly had inflicted in so short a span. It had to be there somewhere but for the life of him he couldn't spot it. He looked behind an oak barely wide enough to hide a broom and realized how foolish he was being. He went another ten feet, and halted in consternation.

Down the stream, the day was shattered by the scream of a girl in mortal terror.

26

Fargo flew. Beyond the cottonwoods was a straight stretch but no Ovaro or the pair on him. In his mind's eye he saw them fleeing for their lives with the man-killer after them.

Worry gnawed at Fargo like a termite at wood. He ran until his chest was ready to burst. Stopping, he doubled over and sucked in deep breaths. He would rest for a minute and go on.

The forest was quiet. He marveled at how quickly the bear had circled the cabin and gone after the Ovaro. It was pure luck the grizzly hadn't spotted him or caught his scent.

The ache lessened and Fargo ran. He kept thinking he would spot Wendy and Bethany around each bend but he didn't. When his exhausted body couldn't take the punishment anymore, he stopped. He was caked with sweat, his lungs in torment. Sinking to a knee, he listened in vain for some sound that would tell him the Brit and the girl were safe. When he recovered sufficiently, he set off again.

A copse of alders blocked his view. He was almost to them when he heard a grunt. Darting to his left to a log, he flattened on the other side. Not a moment too soon.

Brain Eater came out of the alders. Her head was down and she was rumbling in her chest. Dried blood splotched her coat. She went a short way past the log and stopped. Raising her nose to the breeze, she sniffed. Then she sniffed the ground.

Fargo's gut churned. She had caught his scent. If she found him he was dead. The Colt was a man-stopper but all it would do was annoy her.

Brain Eater turned in a circle, still sniffing. She looked south and she looked north. Growling, she lumbered off at a brisk clip, her hump rising and falling with every dip of her enormous body.

Fargo figured she would go as far as the shack, realize her mistake, and come after him. The moment she was out of sight he was up and through the alders. He paced himself, his lungs be damned. It was life or death and he was fond of breathing.

He took pride in his stamina. Not that long ago he'd taken part in an annual footrace that drew some of the best runners in the country, including an Apache girl famed for her fleetness. He didn't win but he came close, and now he called on all his ability to get as far from the griz as he could.

He fretted about the Ovaro, and Beth and the Brit. He hadn't heard shrieks or shots but he hadn't heard any when the man at the shack was killed, either. The stallion's tracks reassured him.

Fargo ran until his legs were mush and his lungs were on fire. Gasping for breath, he shuffled to a boulder close to the water and sat. His hands on his knees, he waited for his body to stop aching. He tried not to dwell on the fact that he was stranded afoot with no food and miles to cover to reach town.

A distant grunt warned him that Brain Eater had taken up the chase.

Fargo rose and made to the south. She would overtake him long before he reached Gold Creek. With just the Colt and the toothpick, killing her was next to impossible.

He could slow her down, though. He swept the ground for a suitable stick and found one about a foot long and as thick as his thumb. He drew the Arkansas toothpick and sharpened one end as he ran.

By the position of the sun he had seven or eight hours of daylight left. Enough to rig several traps. Maybe a deadfall, too, although that would take a lot of doing.

The grizzly was smart but he was smarter. He must believe that more than he believed anything if he was to have any chance at surviving.

From a fork high in an oak Fargo watched to see what would happen.

Grizzlies were sharp-eyed brutes. Brain Eater spotted his bandanna. She stopped and gazed warily about and sniffed. She walked up to it and sniffed some more. She put a front paw on it, unaware that it was stretched over a hole and held in place with small rocks, and that under it was the sharpened stick, embedded deep. She tried to draw back but her own weight worked against her. She yowled as the tip pierced her paw.

Fargo grinned. It wasn't much of a wound but anything that slowed her down helped.

Brain Eater roared. She raised her leg, bit the stick, and wrenched it out. In her rage she shook it and bit it in half. She clawed at one of the pieces and walked in a circle and roared again.

Fargo quickly clambered down. He had a good lead and he wanted to keep it. He jogged for a while, the sun warm on his bare chest. He hadn't liked to give up his buckskin shirt. Fortunately he had a spare in his saddlebags.

A spruce offered his next vantage. He climbed high enough and roosted on a thick limb.

Brain Eater was nearing the next trap. It had been a lot harder to rig but it would hurt her more. Fargo thought she would go right by but his scent on the shirt was strong and her nose didn't fail her. She spied it hanging on what appeared to be a low branch, and stopped.

Brain Eater warily moved toward it. She stopped to sniff and turned her head from side to side. The shirt moved slightly in the breeze. She lumbered closer but stopped again. Fargo began to think she wouldn't be curious enough. Then she raised the same paw and clawed at the shirt.

The principle was simple: a notched limb for a lever, a large log, and gravity. He'd had to strain every sinew to position the log just right.

The grizzly tugged. The shirt moved and the limb was torn out from under the log and the log rolled down on her. She tried to jump over it and once again her weight was her enemy. The log hit hard and she sprawled forward.

Brain Eater was enraged. She attacked the log, biting and clawing. When her fury subsided she turned south again. She was limping.

Fargo scrambled down. He hadn't accomplished much other than making her mad as hell. But she would be more cautious and come on slower, gaining him precious time. The longer he delayed her, the closer he got to Gold Creek and safety.

For about fifteen minutes Fargo held to a steady pace. Another of the innumerable bends brought him to a pool—and two men camped beside it. The flap to their tent was open, and they were seated on stools. Beyond were their hobbled horses.

Fargo figured they were prospectors. "We have to get out of here."

The pair picked up rifles and rose. Both were big and blond and well muscled.

"*Hej,*" one of them said. "*Pratar du svenska?*"

Fargo remembered them now. They were Swedish or Danish. Immigrant farmers, lured to Gold Creek by the bounty. "Brain Eater is after me," he warned. "Take me to town."

They looked at one another.

"*Jag forstar inte,*" the one on the right said.

"*Var snall och prata langsammare,*" said the other.

"Goddamn it." Fargo glanced over his shoulder. They had a few minutes yet. "Do either of you speak English?"

"*Ja,*" the one on the right replied. "*Engelska.*"

"The bear is after me," Fargo explained, and jabbed a finger back the way he had come. "Do you savvy? Brain Eater? She is hunting me and will kill us if we don't light a shuck."

"Bear?" the immigrant on the left said.

"Yes, yes," Fargo said. "Do you understand? Bear. Brain Eater. After me." Again he pointed north.

"Bear," the same man said, and beamed at his companion. "*Bjorn!*"

"*Bjorn?*"

"*Ja.*"

The pair hefted their rifles and eagerly brushed past Fargo.

"What the hell are you doing?"

The one pointed as Fargo had done. "Bear!" he excitedly exclaimed.

"Yes. Brain Eater." Fargo touched his head and made a scooping motion. "Do you understand? The grizzly that has been killing everybody. We must go. Now."

The Swedes looked positively delighted. They raised their rifles.

"No, damn it." Fargo's sense of urgency was climbing. He ran to the nearest man and grabbed him by the shoulder. "Don't do this. Your guns won't stop it." They were armed with old long rifles better suited for small game. "We must get out of here while we can."

The immigrant smiled and nodded. *"Oroa dig inte. Vi kommer att doda bjornen."*

"What?" Fargo said.

"Slappa," the man said.

"What the hell does that mean?" Fargo was growing desperate, and shook him. "You're going to die if you don't listen to me."

"Tillrackligt," the immigrant said, and tugged loose. *"Lamna detta till oss."*

Fargo looked at the other one and the man smiled and nodded. He didn't know what else to do. "You could at least learn the damn language."

"Tack for att bjornen till oss," the man said.

Fargo was about to appeal to them once more but they had run out of time.

Brain Eater was there.

The grizzly barreled around the bend and came to a stop. It looked past the two Swedes at Fargo and let out a growl.

"Run!" Fargo shouted, and dashed to the horses.

As for the immigrants, they grinned and the one on the right said, *"Det ar var tur dag."*

The other one nodded. *"Pengarna ar var."*

Fargo couldn't get the first hobble off. It was a makeshift affair, a short piece of rope with more knots than he had knuckles. He hiked his pant leg and palmed the Arkansas toothpick.

"Vill du skjuta forst?"

"Nej du gar forst."

"Detta var din ide. Det ar ratt att du skjuter forst."

It looked to Fargo as if they were arguing over who should shoot first. He slashed at the hobble but the rope was new and stiff and resisted his blade.

"Behaga. Jag insisterar du gora det."

"Hur omkring om vi skjuter tillsammans sedan?"

A few strands parted but nowhere near enough. Fargo glanced at the grizzly, wondering how long it would continue to just stand there.

Not another second. Brain Eater roared and was on the Swedes with incredible speed. The one on the right bleated, *"God Gud!"* and tried to take aim. A paw crushed his face.

The other Swede cried, *"Han hor dodat dig!"* and fired.

Whether he hit the bear or not was irrelevant; it had no effect whatsoever.

Brain Eater roared as her claws sheared into the second man's crotch. He shrieked and dropped his rifle and cried out.

"Vad du gor du, din dumma bar?"

With a powerful surge, the grizzly ripped him open from man-hood to sternum.

Fargo was only partway through the first hobble. Darting around the horses, he plunged into the woods. He went about ten feet and sprawled flat.

Brain Eater was chomping on the second Swede's innards. His guts had spilled out and the bear had part of an intestine in her mouth and was shaking the ropy coils.

The other man was whimpering and convulsing.

There was nothing Fargo could do. He stayed flat and drew the Colt. It wouldn't do much good but he wasn't going to be ripped apart without a fight.

Brain Eater wolfed a hunk of flesh. Straddling the dead man, she nuzzled his neck and head and sank her fangs into his fore-head. As easily as if she was peeling the crust of a pie, she peeled the scalp from the cranium and spat it out. She licked the blood that welled, then spread her jaws wide and closed them on the man's head. It burst like a melon and she lapped at the oozing brains as if she couldn't get enough of them.

Hampered by the hobbles, the horses were trying to flee and whinnying in panic.

Fargo wished he had the elephant gun. He had a perfect shot.

Brain Eater went to the other Swede. He had stopped moving. She pawed at his body and when there was no reaction, she ripped off an ear and a swatch of hair. Underneath gleamed the skull.

Fargo told himself to look away but didn't.

Brain Eater's teeth were so many razors, slicing through flesh and crunching bone. Once again she indulged in her favorite food and when she was done, she licked the brain pan clean.

The horses had gone about ten yards. One was bucking and struggling to break free of the hobble.

Brain Eater raised her dripping maw. She broke into motion and swiped at the first horse. A leg cracked and the horse squealed and went down. The bucking horse tried to kick Brain Eater but the grizzly dodged and raked her claws from tail to ribs.

Fargo figured she would be busy for a while eating. He crabbed backward and stood. The grizzly was tearing at the second horse's belly. Turning to the south, he stealthily made his way through the woods to the creek.

More running. His feet were sore and his leg muscles protested but he ate up the distance. He wondered how many more hunters or gold seekers he would encounter. Three men had died and he was indirectly to blame. With the bear after him, he invited death on everyone he met.

No sooner did the thought cross his mind than two women came flying up the creek toward him. Both had cornstalk hair and wore plain homespun dresses and bonnets. At the sight of him they stopped and one called out, *"Vem ar du? Var ar vara man?"*

"God in heaven," Fargo blurted. They were the Swedes' wives. He ran to them and they stepped back and thrust out their hands as if in fear of being attacked. "It's not me," he said. "It's Brain Eater."

"Vad han talar om?" the other woman said.

Fargo pointed to the north. "Bear. Do you understand that word?" To get them to understand, he raised both hands and curled his fingers into claws and growled deep in his chest.

"Han ar en galning," the first woman said.

The other one mumbled and then said in atrociously accented English, "Are you crazy man?"

"At last," Fargo said. "Brain Eater is after me. You have to run—"

"Where our husbands?" the woman anxiously asked. "Where Sven? Where Olaf?"

"Dead. Brain Eater killed them and—"

The woman turned to her friend. *"Han sagar vara man ar doda."*

"Vi maste se till ourselves."

To Fargo's amazement, they raced past him. He grabbed at the second woman's arm but she jerked away. "Don't go back there. The bear will kill you, too."

They didn't listen.

Fargo stared after them. That way lay certain death. He stared to the south. That way lay his only hope. He turned north and went after them.

For females in dresses they were remarkably swift. Farming wasn't for the puny, and these two were antelopes. One of them glanced back and said something to the other and both ran faster.

155

"Damn it." Fargo was trying to save their lives. He hoped one would trip so he could overtake them but his luck was true to form.

"Sluta jaga oss!" one of them yelled at him.

The best Fargo could make of it, she had called him a slut or an ass. The first didn't make any sense, and as for the second, he'd been called worse.

The pair were abreast of a wide pine when a gigantic mass of muscle and fur swept from behind it and was on them before either could stop. They screamed in unison and died singly with savage sweeps of the grizzly's paws.

Fargo drew up short. He had tried but they hadn't listened. Whirling, he got out of there. He expected the bear to feast on their brains and that would gain him time. The thud of heavy paws proved otherwise.

Brain Eater was after him.

Fargo willed his body to its utmost. He had already run so far and so hard that he couldn't sustain the pace for long. He was worn out. His hip hurt like hell. His clawed leg hurt worse. But he refused to give up.

As inexorable as an avalanche, Brain Eater closed the distance.

Fargo had one consolation. Bethany had escaped. She was a sweet kid, the kind he'd like to have himself one day, maybe when he was forty or fifty and ready to settle down.

He chuckled at how ridiculous he was being. Here he was being chased by a killer bear and he was thinking of the family he'd never have.

Rocks and boulders covered the ground ahead. He avoided the largest and was almost to bare ground when his left boot became wedged. Momentum carried his body forward and he pitched flat. The pain set his head to spinning. He almost didn't hear the grunt behind him but he did smell the blood and the pungent bear odor. Rising to his knees, he turned.

Brain Eater stood a few yards away. That close she was immense, a mountain of ferocity unrivaled by any creature on the continent.

Fargo's chest constricted. She had him. He could shoot her but he couldn't stop her.

The grizzly whuffed and pawed the earth, her dark eyes glittering with bloodlust. She slavered in anticipation of sinking her teeth into his body.

"Go ahead," Fargo said, his hand on the Colt. "I'll make you pay."

Brain Eater opened her mouth and swept forward. Fargo had the Colt out in a blur and jammed the muzzle into her mouth. He fired just as a tremendous blow cartwheeled him like a feather in a gale. He slammed down close to the creek with one leg in the water. His body pulsed with pain but he made it to his knees again, and he still had the Colt.

Brain Eater was shaking her head. She was bleeding copiously from her mouth, and drops flew all over. She roared, and saw him, and charged.

This was it, Fargo thought. He aimed at her left eye, fired, and missed. The slug scoured a red furrow above it.

She was almost on him. He fired again and her eyeball exploded and then she rammed into him and it felt as if a herd of buffalo were trampling his every bone. Somehow, he stayed conscious. He was on his belly and he had scratches everywhere. He heard coughing. He raised his head and shook it. The fuzziness cleared enough for him to see Brain Eater, doing more head shaking. Blood dribbled from her mouth and the empty socket where her left eye had been.

Fargo grinned. The Colt *could* hurt her. He pushed up and extended the six-shooter. "Come and get it, bitch."

Brain Eater fixed her remaining hate-filled eye on him. Her lips curled from her teeth and she hurtled at him.

Fargo aimed at her other eye. He had to be sure so he didn't shoot until her face was inches from the muzzle.

The blast and her impact were simultaneous. The sunlight blinked out. Pain filled every particle of his body. He felt a crushing weight on his chest and pushed but it wouldn't budge. Gradually he realized it was Brain Eater; she was on top of him. Her hair was in his mouth and nose, her blood on his neck. Spitting and coughing, he twisted his head so he could breathe.

A large shape blotted out the sky.

"Oh God," Fargo said, thinking that the grizzly was getting up.

"No," Wendy said. "Just me and the tyke."

Fargo blinked. The large shape was the Ovaro. The Brit was

dismounting, Bethany in his arm. "Where the hell have you two been?"

"You're the one who told me not to stop until we reached town, remember?" Wendy set Bethany down. "I couldn't do it, though. I couldn't desert you. So we came back."

Bethany squatted and put her hand on Fargo's cheek. "You have the bear on you."

"I noticed."

Wendy was admiring the griz. "Look at the size of this thing. And you killed it without needing my elephant gun. I'm impressed, Yank."

Fargo glared. "My ribs are about to cave in."

"Oh. Sorry."

The Brit tied one end of Fargo's rope to the bear's leg and looped the rope around the saddle horn and goaded the Ovaro. By gradual inches the grizzly slid far enough off that Fargo could wriggle out from under. Wendolyn and Bethany helped him to his feet.

"If you don't mind my saying so, you look like hell."

"Thanks."

Bethany giggled. "You smell like bear pee."

Fargo looked down at himself and sniffed. She was right. He handed his Colt to Wendy and waded into a pool and sat down. The water came as high as his chin. He let it soothe his hurts and aches.

"There's a lot to do yet," the Brit reminded him.

That there was.

They skinned Brain Eater, Fargo doing most of the work since Wendolyn was still weak. They didn't have the salt to cure the hide but that didn't matter. It wouldn't rot before they reached town.

Since Wendy and Bethany had to ride, they couldn't roll up the hide and tie it on the saddle. So Fargo rigged a travois.

It was slow going but they reached Gold Creek about half an hour after the sun went down.

Their arrival caused quite a stir. Everyone came to see the hide and finger the claws. Many snipped hairs as a keepsake.

Mayor Petty was especially pleased to hear that both bears were dead. He called a town meeting in the street and after a long-winded speech about how devoted he was to the public good and how well his plan had worked out, he somewhat reluctantly handed over the bounty.

Fargo and Wendolyn agreed to split it into three equal shares. They looked up the parson and explained the situation and the minister said he knew of a good family that would be happy to take Bethany in.

Fargo didn't think it would be so hard. He squatted and she placed her little hands on his shoulders and looked into his eyes.

"I'll miss you."

Fargo coughed.

Tears trickled down Bethany's cheeks. "I wish I could stay with you. You'd make a good pa."

"No," Fargo said. "I wouldn't."

Bethany hugged him, his face buried against his shirt. She said something he didn't quite hear.

"What was that?"

"I love you."

Fargo pried her loose and nodded at the parson, who picked Bethany up. She was crying.

"Don't worry, my son," the parson said. "She'll be cared for as if she was their own."

Fargo walked out of the church without looking back. Wendy called his name but he kept on walking. He needed a bottle of whiskey. He planned to get drunk and stay drunk for a week or so.

That should be more than enough.

LOOKING FORWARD!
The following is the opening
section of the next novel in the exciting
Trailsman series from Signet:

TRAILSMAN #357
STAGECOACH SIDEWINDERS

*Colorado, 1860—Caught between a rock and a hard place,
Fargo's going to carve out a new trail—with lead.*

A shot cracked sharp and clear from around the next bend in the
winding mountain road.

Skye Fargo drew rein and placed his hand on the Colt at his
hip. A big man, broad of shoulder and chest, he wore buckskins
and a white hat turned brown by the dust of his travels. He heard
shouts and the sounds of the stage that was ahead of him coming
to a stop. Slicking his six-shooter, he gigged the Ovaro to the
bend. He could see without being seen.

Four masked men were pointing six-shooters at the stage. A
fifth had dismounted. The driver's arms were in the air and the
pale faces of passengers peered out the windows.

The fifth bandit swaggered over and opened the stage door.

"Get your asses out here," he barked, "and keep your hands
where I can see 'em."

The first to emerge was a terrified man in a suit and bowler.

He cowed against the coach and fearfully glanced at the outlaws and their guns.

The next was a woman who had to be in her eighties if not older. She held her head defiantly high and when the outlaw took hold of her arm, she shrugged free and said, "Don't touch me, you filth."

The outlaw hit her. He backhanded her across the face and when she fell against the coach, he laughed.

"Leave her be, damn you!"

Out of the stage flew a young tigress with blazing red hair. She shoved the outlaw so hard that he tottered back and then she put her arm around the older woman to comfort her.

The outlaw swore and raised his pistol to strike her.

"No," said a man who wore a flat-crowned black hat and a black duster. "Not her or the old one."

The man on the ground glanced up, swore some more, and lowered his revolver. "Hand over your valuables," he commanded, "and be quick about it."

Fargo had witnessed enough. He didn't like the odds but he couldn't sit there and do nothing. Staying in shadow at the edge of the road, he rode toward them at a walk. His intent was to get as close as he could before he let lead fly but he was still twenty yards out when one of the robbers pointed and hollered.

"Someone's comin'!"

Fargo fired. His shot caught the shouter high on the shoulder and twisted the man in his saddle. Two others started to rein around to get out of there but the man in the black duster and the outlaw on the ground had more grit; they shot back. A leaden bee buzzed Fargo's ear. The man in the duster fired again and Fargo felt a sharp pain in his right leg at the same instant that he put a slug into the outlaw standing by the stage. The man staggered, then recovered and ran to his horse and swung up. Fargo fired yet again but by now all the outlaws were racing up the road. He didn't go after them. He was bleeding.

The driver jerked up a shotgun but the gang was out of range.

Fargo came to a stop next to the stage.

"Don't let them get away!" the terrified man bawled.

Dismounting, Fargo kept his weight on his left leg and hiked at his right pant leg.

"They wing you, mister?" the driver asked.

Fargo grunted and eased down. He pulled his pant leg to his knee. The slug had torn through the flesh of his calf and gone out the other side. "Son of a bitch." Thankfully, though, his bone had been spared. The blood was already slowing.

"Why are you sitting there?" the terrified man demanded. "You should go after them."

"Shut the hell up, Horace," the driver said. "Can't you see he's been shot?"

"Don't you dare talk to me in that tone, Rafer Barnes," Horace said. "I won't have it, you hear?"

Fargo pried at the knot in his bandanna.

A dress rustled and perfume wreathed him. The redhead smiled warmly and said, "Thank you, sir, for coming to our rescue."

"Let me see that leg, young man," the older woman said, sinking to her knees. "I've tended my share of bullet wounds in my time."

"I've been hurt worse," Fargo said, and went to tie his bandanna over the holes. To his surprise and amusement, she slapped his hand.

"Let me see it, I said." She bent and probed and announced, "It's not serious but you'll be limping for a good long while. I advise you to see a sawbones, though, to clean it up."

"Listen to my grandma," the redhead said. "She always knows what she's talking about."

Fargo wrapped his bandanna and tied it. Without being asked, the young woman slipped an arm under his to help him stand.

"There you go." Her green eyes were luminous in the light of the full moon and her lips were as red as ripe strawberries.

Fargo breathed in the scent of her hair. "I'm obliged, ma'am."

"My name is Melissa. Melissa Hart. This is my grandmother, Edna."

The older woman had risen and was brushing off her dress. "How do you do?"

Rafer Barnes leaned down from the seat. "I'm obliged, too,

mister, for the help. I'm not supposed to let you, but how about if you ride up here with me the rest of the way and spare your leg?" He paused. "You're bound for Oro City, I take it?"

Fargo admitted that he was and accepted the offer. His wound was less likely to take to bleeding again than if he rode the Ovaro. He tied the stallion to the back of the coach, limped to the front, and climbed on. The women and Horace were already inside.

Rafer offered his hand. "Those owlhoots would have done us harm if you hadn't come along when you did."

Fargo didn't mention that he had been behind the stage most of the way from Denver. "They'd have robbed you and gone their way." That was how most stage robberies went.

"No sir," Rafer said with an emphatic shake of his stubble. "They'd've shot Horace and me and beat on the ladies as a warnin'."

"What makes you so sure?"

Rafer lashed the team. Under them the stage creaked and rattled. When the horses were in motion he said, "I reckon you haven't heard about the war."

"The what?"

"The *Oro Gazette* is callin' it the Stagecoach War. The company I work for and another are out to be top dog in Oro City and the squabble has become downright vicious."

Fargo had noticed the name of the line when he climbed up. "I've heard of the Colorado Stage Company. What's the name of the other?"

"The Cobb and Whitten Express. It's named after the two gents who own it. Cobb I don't know much about but I've met Whitten and he can be a pushy gent. I reckon he doesn't like competition."

"There's not enough business for two stage lines?" Fargo recollected hearing that a gold strike gave birth to Oro City about a year ago.

"More than enough. The Denver run brings in a heap of money and there are other runs to other towns and mining camps and settlements."

Fargo sat back. His leg was bothering him and he'd like to spend the rest of the ride quiet but Rafer was a talker.

"Yes, sir. Oro City is growin' by leaps. Give it a couple of years and it'll be almost as big as Denver."

Fargo had his doubts. He'd heard that most of the gold was placer with a lot of sand mixed in.

"We've already got nearly as many saloons," Rafer related. "For lendin' a hand back there, I'll treat you to a drink when we get to town."

"Make it a bottle."

Rafer laughed. "I reckon that's fair." He glanced at Fargo. "I should warn you, though. You hit two of them. They're liable to want to get even."

"Do me a favor and keep quiet about it."

"Fine by me but you're forgettin' the folks in the stage. They'll gab. The *Gazette* will hear of it and by tomorrow night everyone in Oro City will know who you are and what you did."

"Hell."

"Sometimes it doesn't pay to be one of those—" Rafer stopped. "What do they call 'em? Good Samaritans?"

The stage lurched up a switchback and Rafer devoted his attention to handling the ribbons. "Easy there," he said to the horses as the wheels rolled dangerously near the edge.

Fargo glanced down. He wasn't bothered by heights but the five-hundred-foot drop to jagged boulders was enough to make anyone's skin crawl.

"Don't worry. We won't go over," Rafer said, and chuckled. "I've been handlin' a stage for more years than you've been alive."

"Is that a fact," Fargo said, still staring over the side.

"It sure enough is. I got my start as a cub on a Boston line years ago and then came west. Been out here ever since." Rafer guided the team around a sharp turn with the skill born of the long experience he claimed. "How about you? What do you do for a livin'?"

"This and that."

"You don't care for me to pry? Fair enough. But if I was to guess I'd say you make your livin' as a scout."

"My buckskins give me away?"

Rafer grinned. "Lots of people wear deer hides. Hunters,

trappers, you name it." He shook his head. "No, I'd peg you for a scout because you have that look scouts have."

"I have a look?"

"Take a gander in a mirror sometime," Rafer said. "It's those hawk's eyes of yours. Like you're lookin' far off when the rest of us can only see up close."

"That makes no sense."

"It does if you're a pigeon and not a hawk," Rafer said, and cackled.

Fargo folded his arms and made himself as comfortable as he could. The wind was chill at that altitude at night even in the summer. Overhead, stars sparkled. To the south a coyote serenaded them.

Rafer breathed in deep and exclaimed, "God Almighty, I love this country."

Fargo shared the sentiment. The mountains and the prairie were as much a part of him as his arms and his legs. He could no more do without the wild places than he could do without women.

"Did you see that?" Rafer asked.

Fargo looked up. They were climbing toward the crest of a ridge. As near as he could tell, the stretch of road to the top was clear. "See what?"

"Up yonder," Rafer said, and pointed at the top. "I saw somethin' move."

"A deer, maybe," Fargo said. Or it could be an elk or a bear or another animal.

"No. I thought I saw the shine of metal. Maybe . . ." Rafer got no further.

The night was shattered by the thunder of rifles. Lead struck the coach with loud *thwacks* and one of the horses whinnied.

Fargo's Henry was in his saddle scabbard. He clawed at his Colt even though the range was too great. "Do you have a rifle?"

Instead of answering, Rafer dropped the ribbons and cried, "I'm hit!"

No other series packs this much heat!

THE TRAILSMAN

Follow the trail of Penguin's Action Westerns at
penguin.com/actionwesterns   S310-110310

"A writer in the tradition of Louis L'Amour
and Zane Grey!"
—*Huntsville Times*

National Bestselling Author

RALPH COMPTON

**Available wherever books are sold or at
penguin.com**

S543-122310